Hurricane Power

Sigmund Brouwer

orca sports

Orca Book Publishers

Library and Archives Canada Cataloguing in Publication

Brouwer, Sigmund, 1959-
Hurricane power / written by Sigmund Brouwer.

(Orca sports)
Originally published: Red Deer, Alta. : Coolreading.com, 1998.
ISBN 978-1-55143-865-8

I. Title. II. Series.

PS8553.R68467H8 2007   jC813'.54   C2007-903144-7

Summary: When David is confronted by angry gang members and malicious
teammates, he finds out what it really means to run for your life.

First published in the United States, 2007
Library of Congress Control Number: 2007928530

Orca Book Publishers gratefully acknowledges the support for its publishing
programs provided by the following agencies: the Government of Canada
through the Book Publishing Industry Development Program and the Canada
Council for the Arts, and the Province of British Columbia through the BC Arts
Council and the Book Publishing Tax Credit.

Cover design: Teresa Bubela
Cover photography: Getty Images
Author photo: Bill Bilsley

Orca Book Publishers   Orca Book Publishers
PO Box 5626, Stn. B   PO Box 468
Victoria, BC Canada   Custer, WA USA
V8R 6S4   98240-0468
www.orcabook.com
Printed and bound in Canada.
Printed on 100% PCW recycled paper.
010 09 08 07 • 4 3 2 1

chapter one

All right, I'll admit it was stupid to point a water pistol—especially one that looked so real—at a complete stranger. But in my defense, I had just bought it as a birthday present for my little brother.

Standing outside the store in the parking lot in the hot afternoon sunlight, I held the dusty old pistol, admiring how it looked. I couldn't believe my luck. I'd found it in the bottom of a bargain bin—priced at next to nothing—in the back of a secondhand store.

Also in my defense, it was only my second day in Florida. Miami, Florida, to be exact. I had just finished my first day of high school, about a block down the street. I didn't know yet that in Miami, people have good reason to be nervous about guns.

You see, I was born and raised in Wawa, a northern bush town in Ontario. People don't get shot at much in Canada. And especially not in Wawa. Up there, if someone saw you holding a gun, they'd look around for a movie camera and stunt men. Or they'd think it was a cheap water pistol that looked just like the real thing. Which, of course, this one was.

That was the third thing in my defense. My gun was only a water pistol.

Anyway, this kid about my age—seventeen—walked past me in the parking lot.

He wore a leather jacket, even though it was hot. He had short dark hair. Dark eyes. He was kind of handsome and he looked really intense.

He glanced at the gun in my hand and froze.

"Hello," I said.

"Come on," he said. "You don't want to be doing that, man." He had a thick accent. I thought the words sounded cool the way he said them: Chu doan wanna be dune dat, mon.

"Doing what?" I asked, still thinking about the way he spoke and wondering if I could mimic the accent for my hockey buddies back home the next time I called.

Then I noticed his eyes were bugging out. I had unintentionally pointed my water pistol at his stomach. That answered my question. He didn't want me to point the gun at him.

"Oh," I said. "This?"

I brought it up to show him that it was only a water pistol. Now it pointed at his chest.

"What you want, man? I got no money. No drugs. Or is this some kind of Black Roses thing?"

Once again I was impressed by his accent. I rolled that sentence around in my mind, liking the sound of it. Maybe I would try to talk like him tonight at dinner when I told my parents and brother about this. After I gave the water pistol to my brother.

The kid brought his hands up. Then I realized I shouldn't be trying to imitate his voice in my mind. He thought this was a stickup. Like at gunpoint.

"No," I said, waving the water pistol, "you don't get it. This is a—"

He didn't give me a chance to finish. He snaked his right hand into his jacket pocket and pulled out a wad of bills.

"Okay, okay," he said. "This is all I got. Take it. Just don't shoot."

Then my eyes bugged out. This was getting serious all of a sudden.

"You don't understand—" I began.

He tossed the money on the pavement near my feet.

I glanced down as the bills scattered. I looked up.

He was already backing away from me.

I had just robbed someone at gunpoint!

An old woman got out of a nearby car. She saw my water pistol. She saw the money on the ground. She saw the dark-haired kid moving away. She screamed, fell back into her car and leaned on her horn. People on the sidewalk at the end of the parking lot stopped and stared. Then they saw the gun. And they screamed too.

The dark-haired kid turned and ran.

"No!" I shouted. I bent down and scooped the bills into my left hand. I still held the pistol in my right hand. "No! Come back!"

I started to chase him. Money waving in one hand. Pistol waving in the other.

He didn't stop.

Neither did I.

He had a fifty-yard head start. And he was fast.

But so was I. At school back in Wawa, kids had called me Greyhound because a big dog had once chased me across the playground. I'd been so scared that it hadn't come close to catching me. I didn't think it was a big deal that people said I was the fastest kid in town. It's like a goldfish being proud that it's the biggest fish in the bowl.

"Come back!" I shouted again, my legs pounding on the pavement. I wore jeans and a T-shirt, but I had on a pair of Nike cross-trainers, so my feet didn't hurt when I ran. And it felt great to push myself. "Stop!"

We ran down a street with small shops on each side. Dozens of people slowly walked along, carrying shopping bags. The kid in front of me slammed into a couple of them, sending them spinning. Each time it happened, he turned back to see me still chasing him. That would send him slamming into other people. By the time they realized what was happening, I was right there to slam into them again. Even though I called out apologies as I sped past, I still heard angry yells and screams behind me.

I figured out that they were responding to the gun in my hand by the time I cleared the last of the people on the sidewalk. I also realized the gun probably wasn't helping me convince the kid that my intentions were friendly.

Finally, I threw the water pistol into the street and just concentrated on trying to catch the kid.

The sidewalk ahead was clear and shaded by palm trees. Now there were houses on both sides of the road. The kid in front of me didn't slow down. I was impressed at how fast he could run.

My breath started to come faster. My heart sounded like a heavy drum banging in my ears.

"Your money!" I shouted. "I just want to give you your money!"

I should have heard the warning siren. But I was running too hard. And concentrating too much on catching the kid.

I didn't see the police car until it swerved onto the sidewalk in front of me. Tires screamed as it skidded to a stop.

I was moving too fast to stop, but the front end of the car blocked the sidewalk.

I smashed into its fender and flipped sideways. Rolling on the grass beside the sidewalk, I saw a big house and lots of wide bushes. I smacked into the bottom of one of those bushes and lay there, gasping.

A split second later, the police car door slammed.

I heard a thump of boots. And then I saw the boots on the ground in front of my eyes. Brown boots, as if that mattered at this point.

"Hands on your head!" a deep voice said. "If I see a weapon, I'll shoot first and ask questions later."

I did as he said. I would not be able to answer questions if I were dead.

Handcuffs clicked around my right wrist first.

Funny, I thought. The Chamber of Commerce brochures didn't say anything about stuff like this.

chapter two

The policeman jerked me away from the bush. Then he pulled me to my feet. I sucked air hard, trying to get my breath back.

I watched the other officer jog down the sidewalk, back toward the stores. A small group of people had begun to gather a short way down the sidewalk.

"Okay, kid," the officer said in a tired voice. He pushed me toward the police car. Its flashing lights blinded me. "What's the deal?"

He was a big man—blond, with a mustache. His dark uniform had darker sweat spots under the arms.

"It was a mistake," I said. "Honest. I can explain."

"Good," he said. He pushed me against the back door of the car. The front door stood open. I could feel cool air flowing from inside. "Hands on the roof."

I put my handcuffed hands on top of the car.

When the policeman kicked my left foot to spread my legs, I nearly fell.

He patted the back of my shirt, under my arms and along the inside of my pant legs.

"Who was the punk you were chasing?" He took a step back from me. I could hear talking from the crowd. "This have anything to do with drugs?"

"No, no, no," I said, still gulping for air. "I was trying to give him back his money."

"Why'd you take it?"

"I didn't," I answered. "He gave it to me."

"Right," he said. He sounded bored, like he'd heard this sort of story a hundred times a day. "He just gave it to you. Like he was tired of carrying it. Did the gun in your hand have anything to do with him giving you his money?"

"Yes," I said. Then I realized how that sounded. "Um, no," I said. "It's just that—"

My head was turned sideways, toward the crowd. I watched as the other officer walked back to us, pushing his way through. He was blond too. No mustache. He had a donut of fat around his middle.

"Punk's heat was just a toy," he said to the policeman behind me. He held it high. I had to admit, it did look real. "The government made these things illegal because of the trouble they can cause. Where'd you get it?"

"Illegal?" I said. "It was buried in a bargain box at the secondhand store and—"

"You see any others?" he asked.

I shook my head no.

"We'll have to keep this," he said. "Besides being against the law, it's just too dangerous to let you run around with a toy that looks so real."

"That's what I was talking about," I said quickly. "The kid saw the gun and—"

"'Aboot'?" the officer who had cuffed me said. "'Aboot'? That sounds like a Canadian accent to me. We get plenty of Canucks down here. You from Canada, kid?"

I hadn't said aboot. I'd said about. But this was no time to argue.

"Yes, sir," I answered. "My family just moved down here yesterday. My dad's a doctor and he's joining a practice in town."

What I didn't add was that he was a doctor who had nearly wrecked his career. And that only a miracle had saved him and our family.

The cop was frowning at me, so I hurried to explain more.

"I bought that water pistol because it's my little brother's birthday. I was standing in the parking lot with it, and the other kid saw it and thought I was pointing it at him. So he gave me his money. I was just trying to give it back to him."

The policeman holding my gun moved up beside us. He sniffed the air.

"You step in something, Frankie?" he asked his partner.

The policeman behind me sniffed the air. "I hope not," he answered. Out of the corner of my eye, I saw him lift his left foot and look at the bottom of his shoe. Then he checked the right shoe.

I sniffed. I smelled it too.

A girl stepped out of the crowd. She had long, straight, brown hair and she wore a red shirt and jeans. She was a little shorter than me but probably about my age. She flashed me a small smile.

"Excuse me, officers," she said. "I go to McKinley High. He's telling the truth. It really was his first day in school. I sat two rows behind him in math class."

One of the policemen sighed. "Frankie," he said, "maybe we should give this kid a break. On account of he's new in town. Besides—you feel like doing two hours of paperwork on this?"

"Over a water pistol? You kidding? The guys wouldn't let us forget about this for a long time."

Frankie sniffed again. He grinned. "Plus, this kid's got enough problems."

"Yeah," his partner agreed. "Too bad this sort of stuff doesn't happen to the perps who deserve it."

I watched as the officer uncuffed my wrists. I turned around, rubbing them one at a time.

"Thanks," I said.

"Forget it," Frankie said. "Just pay attention from now on. You're lucky we didn't shoot when we saw you running down the street waving that pistol around."

They began to get into their car.

"What about the money?" I asked. I counted it quickly. It was mostly one-dollar bills. "There's twelve dollars here."

Frankie's partner shrugged. "You don't know much about this area, do you?"

I shook my head no.

"Let me put it this way," Frankie said. "Someone sees a gun and gives you money that fast, he's probably got a guilty conscience."

"Oh," I said, not really understanding.

"What's your name?" Frankie asked. "Your phone number?"

"David Calvin," I answered. I thought hard about my phone number. I'd only learned it this morning. When I remembered, I gave it to him. He wrote my name and number in his notepad.

"Tell you what," he said. "If that other kid calls in a report about an armed robbery, we'll get in touch with you. In the meantime, keep the money. You'll need it for dry cleaning."

Dry cleaning?

He laughed and shut the car door. The car backed onto the street. Its lights stopped flashing as it pulled away.

"Thanks," I said to the girl. "I think you just saved me a lot of trouble."

I sniffed the air again. I didn't like what I smelled. But I was talking to this pretty girl, and I didn't dare look around.

"It was selfish," she said. "I watched you chase that kid. I saw how fast you guys were running."

I didn't get it. What did running fast have to do with anything?

"Anyway," she said. "I'm glad Dad called off practice today because of a teacher conference. Otherwise I wouldn't have seen how fast you can run."

I must have looked as confused as I felt.

"My name is Jennifer Lewis," she explained. "My dad's the high school track coach. I hoped if I did you a favor, you might do one for me. Would you try out for the track team? We sure could use your help."

"Um, sure," I said. I hadn't thought much about track. I'd always been fast, but in Canada I'd played hockey.

"Come out tomorrow after school," she said. "We meet in the gym. I'll look for you there."

"Um, sure," I said again.

She giggled. "But maybe you should find another shirt before tomorrow."

She pointed at the front of my shirt.

I looked down. My shirt was smudged with dirt and grass from when I had rolled and smacked into the bush.

And then I saw something else—something that explained the smell. Something that looked like peanut butter. But wasn't.

I groaned. If I'd wondered how my first full day in Florida could get any worse, this was the answer.

"I hope your shirt isn't ruined," Jennifer said. "People who don't clean up after their dogs are real jerks."

chapter three

After my last class the next afternoon, I followed the dim hallways of the school to the gym. McKinley High was a two-story stone building, built in the 1930s. I knew that because it said so on a sign near the front doors. The sign also explained that the school had been named after William McKinley. He had been president of the United States from 1897 to 1901. Someone had spray-painted *WHO CARES* over the sign, along with a number of things I'd get in trouble for repeating at home.

It wasn't hard to believe that the school building was that old. The floors had yellowed under dull wax. The lights in the hallway flickered as air conditioners kicked on. The air conditioners rattled like a truck full of empty pop cans. The paint on the gray walls was peeling away.

So I wasn't surprised that the gym had scarred wood floors and an ancient scoreboard that hung above a stage at one end.

I saw a small group of kids at the far end.

I walked over slowly. I wasn't sure I wanted to be here, being new to the school and all. It would have been easier to go straight home and do my homework. Not that I like homework. Back in Wawa, I could have found a hundred different things to do. Here...

Here...I was just paying someone back for keeping me out of trouble.

I put a smile on my face as Jennifer looked up from the group of kids.

A man wearing a red hat concentrated on

something written on his clipboard. His hat looked like the one Elmer Fudd wore in the Bugs Bunny cartoons. In fact, the man kind of looked like Elmer Fudd. Elmer Fudd with a whistle.

"Hello," he said when he noticed me. "You must be David. Jennifer told me about you. She says you could be an all-state runner."

"All-state?" I said. "I don't think so."

"Me neither," a guy beside Jennifer said. He had wavy black hair. He looked like a magazine model: the kind who thinks it's cool to look down his nose at the camera while modeling the type of designer suit that you'd only wear if you liked ballet more than hockey. He turned to Jennifer. "You probably just asked him to join the team because you think he's cute."

"Don't be such a jerk, Jason," she said. "Just because I won't go out with you—"

"That's enough," Coach Fudd said. I corrected that in my head. Coach Lewis. "You two will destroy our team's unity. It's important that you all get along."

Jason turned his head so Coach Lewis couldn't see him. He dramatically rolled his eyes.

"Besides," Coach continued, "we need Jason. Not only is he our fastest runner, but he also helps keep my computer running. That machine's so complicated, I'd be in trouble without him."

Jason seemed to like the coach's compliment. He stopped rolling his eyes and said in a nicer voice, "Hey, Coach? I have an idea. Why don't we run an indoor sprint? That way we can all see exactly how the new guy runs." He shot me a challenging smirk.

I hadn't brought my gym bag with me. I'd actually been thinking about telling Jennifer that I wasn't interested in the track team. It wasn't hockey. But now, of course, I had something to prove.

I gave Jason a big grin. "Sounds like a good idea."

"But you don't have any gear with you," Coach Lewis said to me. "And everybody else has stretched and warmed up."

"That's all right," I said. I just wanted to wipe that smug look off Jason's face. "I'm good to go."

chapter four

Coach Lewis lined seven of us up at one end of the gym. The other six, including Jason, wore gym shorts and T-shirts. I was sure I looked out of place, standing there beside them in my jeans. I suddenly felt self-conscious. Especially with all the girls, including Jennifer, watching us.

What was I doing here? I was about to race six kids I didn't know in a high school I'd attended for only two days. I was doing it because of stupid pride, because some guy had dared me.

Worse, I knew I was a hockey player. That's the only sport I've ever cared about. I wasn't into track. Why did I think I could run against guys who actually competed in track events?

The guys beside me dropped to a crouch. They each placed one heel against the wall behind us.

Huh?

"David," Coach Lewis said. "Get set."

"I am set," I said, feeling more out of place. I decided that even if these guys smeared me, I was going to do my best. But I wished I knew what the coach was talking about.

"In the blocks, set," he said.

"Um, blocks?" I said.

Jason laughed, which instantly made me feel mad again. Now I understood why I had decided to race him.

"You'll get a better jump from a crouched position," Coach Lewis said. "Use the wall behind you in place of starting blocks."

Starting blocks? I guess I should have

known. But my school in Wawa wasn't big on track. And I'd never watched it on television.

"I'm okay this way," I said. Coach Lewis was probably right. But I'd never used blocks before, let alone a wall. I didn't think this was a good time to risk trying something that could cost me time.

"Your choice," Coach Lewis said.

He looked at the others. "To the end of the basketball court," he said. "Any questions?"

No one had questions.

Coach Lewis nodded. He brought his arm up.

"Take your mark..."

I felt the adrenaline start to pump.

"Set..."

A fraction of a second later, Model Guy was pushing off from the wall.

"Go!"

Coach dropped his arm as he shouted. Jason had jumped out ahead of the rest of us. This was no time, though, to stop and point out that Jason had cheated. Instead I focused on my legs, which were pumping as fast as they could.

A quarter of the way across the gym floor, I felt this wonderful balloon of excitement growing inside me. The thunder of shoes on the hardwood only added to the thrill. The weirdest part of all was that I didn't feel my own feet on the floor. I was in full motion, and it felt like I was breaking free of gravity.

I pulled ahead of three guys.

Halfway across, I pulled ahead of two more.

The only person ahead of me was Jason. The other end of the gym seemed to rush toward me.

I still felt totally free, almost outside of my body in the joy of racing hard.

I pushed myself, loving the rhythm of my legs and arms and the feeling of speed. And just like that, I passed Jason. Then I crossed the line at the end of the basketball court.

Cheering and applause broke into my little zone of concentration. Time slowed down. And there I was, hands on my knees, gasping for breath as Coach Lewis walked toward me. He had a huge grin on his face.

"Wow," he said. "Do you have any idea how fast you are?"

I shook my head. I was a hockey player.

"Let me put it this way," he said. "We need you on this team. Will you join?"

We need you. That sounded nice, being new to the school and all. It wasn't like I had any other plans; all my friends were a couple of thousand miles to the north.

"Sure," I said to Coach Lewis. "I'd be happy to."

"Good," he said. "We practice after school every day but Friday. Our first track meet is Saturday. Can you make it?"

"I'll have to check with my manager and booking agent," I joked.

"Huh?" he said. The way his face wrinkled, he looked even more like Elmer Fudd than before.

"Nothing," I said. "Dumb joke. There's nothing to stop me from being there."

Or so I thought at the time.

chapter five

I spent a lot of time and energy learning how to use starting blocks at my first practice. Afterward, Jennifer caught up to me in the hallway.

"Where're you going?" she asked, smiling. We were alone, walking past empty classrooms.

"Home," I answered. Our big old house was half a mile from the school. It wasn't much to look at, but Mom was into interior design. She planned to fix the house up and make it look like something from the 1920s.

"I wanted to ask you about that," she said. "Your home, I mean. There's something I don't understand."

"What's that?" I asked.

"It just seems strange..." She looked at her feet and then back at me. She had a nice smile. "Maybe it's none of my business, but can I ask you a kind of personal question?"

"I guess so."

"Well," she said, "this isn't the nicest neighborhood. Or the nicest school. You've probably figured that out."

I nodded.

The school, for example, had a metal detector at the main entrance. The kind used at airports to make sure people don't take guns or knives onto airplanes. Security guards made sure all students walked through the metal detector. It didn't take much to figure out this place wasn't exactly kindergarten.

All the houses in the neighborhood were really old. Most of them were falling apart. I knew from listening to Mom and Dad that many of these big old houses held four or five families.

"So," Jennifer said, "your family moved down here from Canada. That must have cost your folks a lot of money."

"Probably," I said. "We flew down and hired movers to bring our furniture by truck."

"That's what seems strange to me," she said. "Anybody with any kind of money wouldn't choose to live in this neighborhood or go to this school. So why...?"

"Why am I here? Why did my family move here?"

It was her turn to nod.

"I ask my Mom and Dad that every day." I grinned to show her I wasn't totally serious. Actually I had stopped asking why after they had sold our house in Canada. By then, no amount of arguing could have changed their minds, so I had given up.

"And?" she asked.

"Let me tell you the short story," I said. The long story was something I didn't really want anyone to know. "My dad's a doctor.

He decided he wanted to spend some time helping people who couldn't afford medical care. So he took a two-year leave of absence from his job in Canada and moved us down here so he could work in an inner-city clinic."

She thought about that for a moment. Then she said, "I'll bet the long story is interesting."

Interesting? How about scary and sad? How about something that nearly tore our family apart? And nearly put my dad in jail. But I wasn't going to tell her about that.

"Let's stick with the short story," I said.

I could tell from the look on her face that she wasn't going to give up. So I changed the subject.

"What about you?" I asked. "Your dad..."

"My dad." Her smile got smaller. "He's great. He's taught here and coached the McKinley Hurricanes track team for more than twenty years. When he joined the staff, this was a nice neighborhood. He'd really like to work in a better school now, but people in the school system think he's a loser. Which really hurts. I mean, he cares more about kids than about winning. Around here, though, a track coach needs a winning team to get noticed. And, as you can imagine, this school doesn't attract a lot of star athletes. It's been a long time since we've won a track meet."

She clutched her books to her chest as if she were hugging the slightest chance to help her father.

"That's why I wanted you to join the team as soon as I saw how fast you can run," she said. "Dad's getting close to retirement, and I'd love him to have a winning season. Maybe then he could get a job in a safer school for his last few years of teaching."

"Oh," I said.

Before I could say anything else, Jason caught up to us.

"Jennifer," he said, "your dad wants to talk to you."

Jason smiled at me—a fake-looking smile that we both knew he didn't mean. "Nice run today."

For a second, I felt like knocking his teeth in. But I thought of all I had learned in the last few years because of what my dad had gone through. I knew that Jason and I could be friends or enemies. And it would be a lot easier on both of us if we weren't enemies.

"Look," I said, "in Canada, I played hockey and—"

"You trying to impress me?" he asked.

"No," I said, "I just wanted you to know that I've been part of a team. And I can see that you're good. Now we're on the same team. Maybe we can work together."

I stuck out my hand, hoping he would shake it.

He kept his fake smile in place and walked away, ignoring my hand. Jennifer shrugged and followed him back toward the gym.

It made me mad, of course. I stayed mad as I walked. Until something took my mind off Jason.

Halfway down the hall, I walked past an open corridor. I saw someone standing at the far end. He looked just like the kid who had handed over his money the day before.

"Hey!" I shouted.

His head snapped toward me.

I was right. It was the same guy!

But before I could say another word, he turned and ran. He sprinted down another hallway. By the time I got to where he'd stood, there was no sign of him anywhere.

Weird, I thought. What's got him so scared?

chapter six

"How was your second day of school?" Mom asked me.

We were all sitting at the kitchen table, eating a mushroom, pineapple and tomato pizza.

"Interesting," I said.

"As interesting as your first day?" Dad sniffed the air. "At least you didn't roll in any—"

"Sweetheart," my mom said quickly to him, "we're eating."

"Right," he said. He grinned at her. As always, I was glad to see them getting along. A year ago, things had been different. A lot different. But seeing them together now was like seeing a pair of newlyweds.

Mom's a redhead, with a few strands of gray starting to show up. She had on a blue T-shirt stained with paint from the work she'd started in a hallway. Dad had not changed from his white dress shirt and tie; he had a paper towel tucked into his shirt to protect it from tomato sauce. He kept his dark hair short, almost a buzz cut. People say that I look a lot like him—not skinny, not chunky, medium height, brown eyes and a chin with a dimple right in the middle.

"So define 'interesting,'" Mom said. "I mean, in terms of your second day at school."

"Well—" I stopped myself. Kirk, my six-year-old brother, was about to grab a slice of pizza that had my name all over it.

"Kirk," I said, "is that an alligator outside?"

Kirk's eyebrows shot up as he turned to

look out the window. He's a little redheaded guy with a grin a mile wide. I like him a lot. But then, I like pizza a lot too. I made a quick grab for the pizza slice.

"Cut it in half and share," Dad said. "And don't mess with your brother like that."

Kirk glared at me for tricking him.

"Come on," I answered. "I'm just trying to help him learn about real life. Some day politicians will be trying to fool him too. Without this kind of lesson, how will he understand democracy?"

"Cut it in half," Dad said.

"Sure," I said, not too upset. At least Dad was around the house now and cared about what I did or didn't do.

"Define 'interesting,'" Mom prompted again.

In between bites of pizza, I told them about Coach Lewis and the short race in the gym and learning how to use blocks. The great thing about the renovation work Mom had started was that she didn't have time to cook. That meant we ate less health food—steamed carrots and broccoli—and more junk food.

My parents thought it was great that I was going to be competing in the track meet on Saturday. I also told them about seeing the kid from the day before.

"The boy you held up at gunpoint?" Dad asked.

"Yeah," I said, not happy with the way that sounded but unable to deny it.

Dad continued, "The boy you were chasing when the cops showed up and made you roll in the—"

"Sweetheart!" Mom cut him off. "Can't you think about anything else?"

"Actually, no," he said. "Everyone at work thought it was hilarious."

"Thanks for sharing it with everyone, Dad," I said.

"Go on with your story," Mom urged.

"Well," I said, "he saw me and ran away."

I put up my hand to stop Dad from interrupting me. "No, I didn't chase him again. No, I didn't roll in—"

"David!" Mom exclaimed.

I grinned at Dad. He grinned back.

"Anyway," I said, "now I know he goes to

McKinley. So if I'm lucky, I'll be able to find him again. I really want to give him his money back—and tell him it wasn't a real gun."

I took a short time-out to gulp down some milk. "What I can't figure out," I said, "is why he hasn't called the police. Or why he didn't at least give me a chance to talk to him today."

"Do you think the fact that you threatened him with a gun might have something to do with his not wanting to talk to you?"

"Dad," I said, "yesterday, when he was running away, he had to see that the police stopped me and cuffed me. And today, he could have called the school security guards. I couldn't have done anything to him. But he didn't ask for their help. It's like he's afraid of them."

I stopped, listening to what I had just said: *It's like he's afraid of them.*

"That's not good," Dad said. His smile was suddenly gone. "Only people who have something to hide work hard to avoid the police. And if he has something to hide..."

He didn't need to finish his thought.

Whatever this kid was hiding couldn't be good. He thought I had robbed him. And now he knew we went to the same school.

Mom's smile had disappeared too. "David," she said, "you be careful."

"Of course," I said. "There's nothing to worry about. Really."

chapter seven

Naturally, the next morning it took all of three hours to bump into him. And his two friends. Two big, mean-looking friends with nose rings and tattoos.

We were in the hallway during the mad rush of kids pushing to get to their classes at the 11:00 AM break. I was on my way from my American history class to math class. I was thinking about the lesson I'd just had on the War of 1812. I had learned about it in Canada too. The short version of it is that the Americans lost to their neighbors north of the border. Of course the history teacher here had taught about it differently. She said that the Americans had not succeeded in winning.

Still, it was interesting, the way history can be when you look at the stories instead of just memorizing dates. Like how British warships were so close to destroying Washington, DC, that when night fell, a lot of Americans wondered if the White House would still be standing in the morning.

Of course back then it wasn't called the White House. It got that name after it had to be painted with whitewash; the outside had been scorched by a fire that almost destroyed it. And when the sun rose the morning after the battle, the Americans could still see the flag. It waved in the shrouds of cannon smoke that hung in the air like fog. That inspired Francis Scott Key to write a little poem that started, "Oh, say, can you see, by the dawn's early light, what so proudly we hailed at the twilight's last gleaming?"

I guess, if you're an American, that little poem can give you the shivers. But when I hear it as a Canadian, I remember that the Americans definitely did not win the War of 1812. And I've noticed they haven't tried to fight us since. Of course that wasn't something I was going to bring up on my third day of school in Florida.

I was thinking all of this and smiling to myself when I nearly bumped into the kid from the water pistol stickup. He had been walking toward me with his head down.

I stopped. He stopped. He brought his head up. Our eyes met.

I put my hands up to stop him getting past me.

"Look," I said. "I want to talk to you about—"

"You leave me alone," he said. "I don't want to talk. I don't want nothing to do with you."

"I just want a chance to explain," I said. I dug around in my pocket to get out some money. I hadn't forgotten that I still owed him twelve dollars.

That's when the two big guys stepped in front of him. I hadn't noticed them in the crowd of people talking, laughing and hurrying to get to their next classes.

One of the guys grabbed my arm and squeezed hard. It felt like a lion had gripped my arm in its jaws. "Don't try nothing," he said.

"But—"

Students flowed around us, ignoring us, like rushing water around boulders in a stream.

"Back off, Jack," the other one said. He wore a black T-shirt with the sleeves ripped off. There was a tattoo of a black rose on his left bicep.

A black rose? Hadn't this kid said something about a black rose when I had held him up with the water pistol?

"If Carlos says he don't want to talk," the other tattooed guy said, "then he don't want to talk."

Math was not my best subject, but I could count. Three against one. This was probably not the best time to argue.

"Sure," I said. "No problem."

I held my breath, wondering what would happen next.

Nothing. The first guy let go of my arm. The second guy pushed me aside. And all three of them walked away and melted into the crowd.

Being born with more stubbornness than brains, I couldn't quite leave it at that. First, it really bugged me that this kid thought I was a thief. Second, I wanted to give him his money back. Third, if he had friends like that, I didn't want him as an enemy. And fourth, I was curious. After all, it was strange that he didn't seem to care that I had pulled a pistol on him. It was even stranger that he hadn't told his buddies to do something to me once I was caught.

All I wanted was to know who he was. Maybe I could find him later, when he was alone, and give him his money back. Just so I wouldn't have to keep worrying about it.

I decided to follow them.

That part was easy. There were so many students in the narrow hallway that all I had to do was stay a couple of steps back. Not once did any of them turn around.

I stayed with them until I saw the kid walk into a classroom.

I wrote his name and the room number down on a piece of paper: *Carlos, Room 225—Wednesday, 11:00.*

I knew his first name as well as the room number, day and time of one of his classes. The information I had just written was almost enough to track him down—without his buddies. But for the rest of my plan to work, I would have to wait until I could talk to Jennifer at the end of math class, which was my next class, and I was already late.

chapter eight

"Um, Jennifer," I said. "Could you do me a favor?"

Math class had just ended. I got to her desk as she stood up. Her hair was pulled back in a ponytail.

"What do you need?" she asked.

"Remember the dumb thing I did a few days ago? You know, with the water pistol?"

She started to laugh. "Yeah. And I remember that you asked me not to tell anyone in school about it. And I haven't, if that's what you're worried about."

I shook my head. "No, I didn't think you would break a promise."

Students squeezed past us in the narrow aisle between the desks. They were all in a hurry. There wasn't much time before the next class.

"He goes to McKinley," I said. "The guy that I robbed...I mean, the guy who gave me his money because he thought—"

She laughed again. "He goes to school here? Is he going to call the cops and have you tackled in the hallway? Of course, if he did, you wouldn't have to worry about landing in—"

"He hasn't called the cops," I said, cutting her short. Like I needed to be reminded once more of what I had accidentally landed in. "That's what's strange. And he wouldn't give me a chance to apologize."

Jennifer looked at the clock on the wall of the classroom.

I took the hint and started walking her toward the door.

"Anyway," I said, "I'm hoping you can help me find him."

"Me? I didn't even get a good look at his face," she said. She crinkled her forehead. "How can I help you find him?"

"Actually," I answered, "I need your dad's help. You see, I know the kid's first name is Carlos, and he went into room 225 at eleven o'clock. Maybe, with that information, your dad could get me his class schedule. It'd be even better if I could get his full name and address. That way I can track him down and give his money back. I know the teachers here are all hooked up on computers and—"

"Ancient computers," Jennifer said, "donated by a company that was going to throw them out. And Dad's not too good with computers. He relies on Jason to help him."

"Well," I said, "maybe your dad can figure out how to get into the system."

She kept frowning as we walked into the busy hallway.

"Why not just wait for him after class?" she asked.

"His class is way across the school. I'll never get there in time to catch him coming out. Watching him go in made me late to class today. Besides," I added, "he's got these friends. More like bodyguards. It doesn't seem like they're going to let me get close to him at school. And he keeps running away. If I can talk to him at his home..."

"Boy," she said, "these days people are pretty strict about privacy things. I'm not sure my dad would even give you information about another student."

I should have thought of that. After all, the school had a metal detector and security guards.

Jennifer stopped. She smiled suddenly, erasing the crinkle of her forehead. "I have an idea," she said. "The perfect reason for Dad to try to find out more about Carlos."

I didn't have an idea, so I just waited for her to tell me hers.

"You didn't catch him, right?" she asked. "That means he's really fast."

"I was getting close," I said, unable to stifle my pride. "If the cops hadn't shown up—"

"Sure," she said. "Sure." She giggled while I sulked.

"Someone that fast could help our track team," she said. "With you and Carlos running with Jason, we'd have a serious shot at winning. Once I tell Dad about Carlos, I'm sure Dad will look up his last name and address."

"That's a great idea," I said.

I dug into my back pocket for the slip of paper that had Carlos's room number on it. Folding the paper, I handed it to Jennifer. She put it into the front pocket of her jeans.

That's when someone pushed me so hard from behind that I almost fell into the lockers.

I turned around.

Jason glared at me. He held up his fists, ready to take a punch at me.

"Leave my girl alone," he said.

"Huh?" I said.

"I saw you give her a note." He stepped toward me. I didn't back away. Jennifer stepped between us.

"Jason," she said, "don't. He didn't give me that kind of note. And I've been telling you for a long time that I'm not your girl."

Jennifer turned to me. "Leave," she said. "I'll handle this."

I didn't want to leave. I wasn't a chicken. Nobody was going to scare me away.

"Just leave," she said. "Please? If you guys fight, you'll both get kicked off the track team. And you guys are the one-two runners. The team needs you. My dad needs you."

"Sure," I finally said.

I left them there, arguing.

Why did life have to be so complicated?

chapter nine

After school, I realized I was not looking forward to track practice. Instead of being a place to make friends, it seemed like it was going to be just the opposite.

Jason was the team ringleader. After I beat him, he made it obvious that he thought I was a jerk. So everyone else treated me like I was one too. Except for Jennifer, no one else had talked to me during practice yesterday.

After five minutes in the locker room, things didn't seem any different. I said hello to a few of the guys as we all began to change into gym clothes. I didn't get much more back other than grunts.

I thought about my hockey buddies up in Canada. There, sitting around before practices and games had been half the fun. Playing the game was the other half of the fun. And sitting around after the game was the other half. I know a math teacher would say three halves of fun add up to more than they should—but that math teacher had never belonged to our team.

Here, I was ignored as I pulled my gear out of my locker. Coach Lewis had assigned it to me at my first practice, and I'd dropped off my gear before classes. I was ignored as I dressed. And I was ignored as I walked to the gym with the rest of the team.

Fine, I told myself, I can live without them. I'd stay on the team only because I had made a promise. And I'd show all of them who was the fastest runner. Today. Tomorrow. And every day after that.

* * *

"Split up and go to your areas!" Coach Lewis barked.

We had finished stretching and warming up in the gym. Coach had then sent us outside to the field. The breeze was humid and smelled a little of salt; it was coming from the ocean. I wished for a moment that I was out on the beach instead of feeling so lonely among all these people.

I began to walk toward the track. Others headed for the high-jump area. The long-jump pit. The shot-put area.

Jennifer caught up to me.

"I've asked Dad to look up Carlos's address," she said. "He sounded pretty excited about finding another sprinter. With the address, you can talk to Carlos anytime you want. If you're lucky, he won't have those big guys with him."

"Thanks," I said.

"Gotta go!" She jogged past me, heading to the high-jump bar.

Someone hit me with his shoulder.

Jason. He jogged by, acting like it was an accident.

I took a deep breath to keep from getting angry. Maybe later Jennifer could tell me what this was all about. Although I had a pretty good idea.

Jason was waiting for me on the track at the starting blocks. He gave me a big grin that I didn't believe was for real.

"Hey, turtle," he said. "Anyone tell you yet that I let you beat me yesterday in the gym?"

I ignored him.

"Anyway," he said, "I've got twenty bucks that says you lose our next sprint."

All the other guys in the sprint gathered around.

I didn't say anything.

"Chicken?" Jason asked.

The others were smirking, just like Jason. Five of them, all skinny like racing dogs. All wearing track shorts and T-shirts.

"Keep your twenty," I said. "It'll hurt you bad enough when I win."

"Win? You'll finish last. I guarantee it."

He laughed. So did the others.

"Tell you what," I said. "If I win, you quit bothering Jennifer."

That shut him up for a second.

"If you lose to me," he snarled, "you quit the track team."

"Fine," I said. What was it about this guy that made me get mad so easily? And why did I lose all common sense when he made me mad?

Jason high-fived a few of the guys around him. I guess that's when I should have started worrying.

chapter ten

Coach Lewis walked up to us.

"All right, men," he said. "I can only take five sprinters to Saturday's meet. There are seven of you. What we'll do is simple. Each week we'll have a sprint. The top five go to the meet; the slowest two don't. That way, if you miss one week, you'll have a chance the following one. And none of you in the top five will get lazy about keeping your spot. Any questions?"

None.

"Good," Coach Lewis said. "This will be a practice run. It will give each of you a good idea where you stand and how much work you need to do. Tomorrow you'll race to see who competes in the meet."

He lined us up in the blocks. I fingered the small silver cross that hung around my neck and concentrated on what I'd learned the day before. Crouch, rise, push off. A lot of our training time had been spent on form. Shaving a tenth of a second off at the blocks might mean the difference between first and last.

As Coach Lewis jogged to the finish line, Jason spoke to me out of the side of his mouth.

"Hey, loser," he said. "Remember our little deal. I don't expect to see you here tomorrow."

What he didn't know was that he couldn't say or do anything to make me afraid of him. Not after what I'd gone through with my dad the year before.

"Keep talking," I said. "You'll just make me run faster."

He laughed. So did the others. Again, I should have wondered why.

Coach Lewis was now a hundred yards away. He had his stopwatch in one hand and a starter pistol in the other.

"Take your mark...," he called out.

We moved into a ready position in the blocks.

"Set..."

We got set.

Bang!

I was up and running!

I didn't look to either side. I pumped my arms. My whole world became a tunnel of motion, a tunnel that sucked me forward as I seemed to fly.

I'd never really known how fast I could run until yesterday, testing myself against the others. It had seemed so easy and natural to pull away from them. That had amazed me.

This time was no different.

Out of the corners of my eyes, I saw no motion. No other flying arms or pushing legs that signaled I was losing ground. I easily held my spot in the lead.

Twenty-five yards. A heartbeat later, thirty.

Then...

PAIN. Shooting pain in the balls of my feet.

I stumbled, not understanding what had happened.

But I wanted to win so badly, my legs kept pumping. They seemed to be working apart from the message of pain in my brain.

Fifty yards. Sixty...

It felt like someone was jabbing knives into my feet. The harder my feet hit the ground, the harder the knives stabbed me.

But I wasn't going to quit.

The pain began to make me angry, so angry that I screamed.

But I kept running. I let the anger push me into a rage that drove me harder.

Seventy.

I saw someone reaching me on the left. Then on the right.

I screamed louder. Pushed harder. More pain. Sharp, killing pain on the bottoms of my feet.

Eighty...

Ninety...

I screamed again.

A hundred yards. I finished first, barely ahead of Jason.

But the pain drove me to my knees. I let myself fall, skinning my knees on the track. I rolled over and over and over, feeling the track shred the skin off my shoulders and elbows.

When I finally came to a stop, I took a couple of deep breaths.

My feet felt like I'd been running on nails.

I pulled off my shoe and saw blood.

I turned the shoe over. And I saw three thumbtacks that had been pushed into the sole.

In a flash, I understood.

Someone had gotten into my locker. Someone had put tacks in my shoes. It wasn't until the pounding of the sprint that I had driven them through the soles and into my feet.

It didn't take too much brainpower to

figure out who had done it. And that a bunch of the others knew about it too.

My first thought was to show the shoe to Coach Lewis.

My chance came as he walked toward me with a worried look on his face.

"You all right?" Coach Lewis asked.

Behind him I could see the other guys. They were smirking. Like they had just played a great trick on me. It made me angry all over again. So my second thought took me somewhere else.

I wanted to bury those smirks. I saw only one way. And it wasn't by whining to Coach Lewis. Even though I desperately wanted to throw off my second shoe, I didn't. Instead I put the first one back on.

I stood and smiled at Coach Lewis.

"I'm fine," I said. My guts felt like they were ripping in half thanks to the pain in my feet. "I'm going to have to work on my finish, I guess. Falling isn't such great form."

Behind him I saw all those smirking expressions turn to disbelief. Disbelief that I had actually put the shoe back on. Disbelief that I was standing there like it didn't hurt at all.

"Good thing you won the race before you fell," Coach Lewis said.

"Yeah," I said. "Good thing."

As much as it hurt to stand on those tacks, it was worth it to watch those guys stare at me in shock.

"Coach," I said, "do you mind if I sit down and take a breather?"

I'd take the tacks out when he wasn't looking. I didn't want him involved in something that was between Jason and me.

"No problem," he said.

I walked toward a bench beside the track. It hurt more than I can describe, pushing my feet down on the tacks again and again, step by step.

Call me stubborn. Call me stupid. But when some of the guys started clapping, it was worth every step.

chapter eleven

Jennifer's phone call caught us halfway through supper. Unfortunately, Dad got up from the table to answer the phone.

"It's for you," he said, holding the phone out. "Some girl named Jennifer. And after only a few days at school. Wow."

He said it loud enough for Jennifer to hear him.

I swallowed my mouthful of soft-shell taco and groaned. "Thanks, Dad," I said, grabbing the phone. He missed my sarcasm.

"No problem," he said.

I rolled my eyes and sighed. I put my hand over the mouthpiece—like he should have done.

"By the way," I said, "it's not what you think. It's not a big deal that she called."

And it wasn't what Jason thought either. Although I wished, in a way, that it were.

I took my hand off the mouthpiece.

"Hello," I said.

"Hello," Jennifer said. "I'm glad your dad was impressed. Does it usually take you longer than a few days to get a girl to call?"

"Very funny," I said.

"Actually it is." She laughed.

I didn't. I was steamed. More at Dad than at her though.

"Anyway, 2515 Palmetto," she said.

"What?" I said.

"The address is 2515 Palmetto," she said. "And his name is Carlos Pelayo."

The kid's name and address. Dad had rattled me so much that it took me a second to figure out what she was talking about.

"Thanks," I said when I'd gathered myself together. "You were fast."

"Let's go tonight," she said.

"Where?" I said.

"To visit Carlos Pelayo at home. Where else?"

"You want to go with me?" I asked, feeling glad she wanted to be my friend.

"I just want to help my dad with the track team," she answered. "The sooner we go, the better."

"Oh." Maybe she didn't want to be friends.

"Besides," she added, "what are friends for?"

"Oh." Maybe she did want to be friends.

"Well?" she asked. "When should I pick you up? I've got my dad's car."

"Hang on," I said.

I put my hand over the receiver again.

"Mom, Dad," I said to them at the supper table, "you mind if I go out for about an hour?"

"With Jennifer?" Dad asked, grinning.

"It's not like that," I said.

"Right," he said.

"Where are you going?" Mom asked.

"To tell the kid who thought I pulled a gun on him that I'm sorry. Jennifer's got his name and address."

Mom frowned instantly. "Didn't you say that if he's the type who's afraid of the police, maybe he's someone to stay away from?"

I had said something like that. Naturally, my mother would remember.

"I'll be with someone who knows the area," I said. "She wouldn't take me anywhere unsafe."

After a second, Mom nodded. "Finish your dinner first. And be back in an hour, or I'll start to worry."

"Yeah," Dad said, "and introduce us to Jennifer."

I sighed again. I got back on the telephone and told her I'd need another fifteen minutes or so. Then I gave Jennifer our address. I told her I'd be waiting outside on the sidewalk.

"Why the sidewalk?" she asked. "Don't you want me to meet your family?"

I sighed one more time.

chapter twelve

She drove a Ford Escort—a few years old, with a few years' worth of dents. A few years' worth of hot sun had faded the red paint to something that looked pink beneath the streetlights. She drove carefully while talking about nothing much. That was fine with me. I liked the sound of her voice.

The neighborhood we drove to was not at all what I had expected. Around our school—where I had expected Carlos to live—the streets were cluttered with old cars.

As Jennifer drove, the streets got wider. Nicer cars were parked in long driveways that led to large houses with big yards.

I thought of Wawa, my little town of a few thousand people in northern Ontario. Basically it had just one main street. The most famous thing about Wawa was a giant statue of a goose. And even that wasn't real famous. There were no palm trees in Wawa but there were lots of spruce and pine. No Mercedes and BMWs but lots of pickup trucks. In Wawa, the nearby water was not the warm Atlantic but the cold and dark and deep Lake Superior. I wondered what my friends were doing tonight while I cruised in the balmy, calm, night air of southern Florida.

"What a surprise," Jennifer said, breaking into my thoughts. "I wouldn't have guessed Carlos came from a neighborhood like this. Most of the time, if people have money they send their kids to a private school. Not to one like ours."

"Maybe his dad is like mine," I said, blurting out my thoughts.

"Like yours?"

Jennifer had just met Mom and Dad and my brother Kirk. They had gotten along fine, mostly because they'd all had a good laugh as Jennifer told them about watching me roll under a bush. And about discovering the stuff on my shirt.

"Oh yeah, you told me your dad wanted to help people who couldn't afford good medical care. What made him decide to do that?"

"Long story," I said, thinking back to how hard everything had been a couple of years earlier.

"Come on," she said. "You said that to me once before. Are you trying to hide something?"

I was. But I didn't even want her to know that much.

"Look," I said, pointing. "That's his address."

She slowed down at number 2515.

We stared at the huge house, built in the Spanish style. Lights on the lawn pointed upward, throwing the house into a dazzling white display of marble columns and high walls.

"Boy," Jennifer said, whistling in admiration, "living in a place like that, I don't think he needs his twelve dollars back."

I nodded. It made me feel less worried too. Dad and I had been wrong. Carlos wasn't some criminal type who was afraid to call the police. He was a rich kid who didn't miss the money he had given me.

At least that's what I thought, until the front door opened a minute after we rang the doorbell.

chapter thirteen

"Yes?" the woman who answered the door asked, obviously surprised to see us.

She carried a small white dog in her arms. She wore a pink housecoat and had a pink towel wrapped around her head. She had on enough gold to fill an Egyptian pharaoh's tomb. Necklaces, bracelets, rings and earrings. Her skin was as tanned and tough as a mummy's too. Her wrinkles were so deep, I was willing to bet that if she stood outside in the rain, her face would collect water. I had a quick mental picture of her shaking her face, like a big, old, slobbery Saint Bernard. I bit my lip to keep from laughing.

"Good evening," Jennifer said. "We're here to speak to Carlos."

A few other thoughts were going through my mind. This woman definitely wasn't Carlos's mother. I also doubted she was his grandmother. Carlos looked more Hispanic than she did. Maybe a visitor? Maybe Carlos had been adopted by this family?

"Carlos?" she repeated in a scratchy voice.

"Yes, ma'am," Jennifer said. "Carlos Pelayo. We go to school with him. We'd like to invite him to try out for the track team."

"I don't understand," she said.

I couldn't take my eyes off her. Her eyebrows were plucked into a thin high arch, and she had tons of makeup around her eyes. The smell of her perfume was enough to kill a skunk. Her dog lifted its lip to snarl at me, as if it knew my thoughts.

"Well," Jennifer said, "we saw him run the other day. And he's very fast."

No kidding, I thought.

"My dad's a track coach," Jennifer continued, "and we're hoping he can join—"

"I understand that part," the woman said sharply. "What I don't understand is why you're here."

"To speak to him," Jennifer explained patiently.

"Don't treat me like a child," the woman said. "He's not here."

"Oh," Jennifer said. "Maybe you could give him a message—"

"Young lady, he doesn't live here."

What?

"What?" Jennifer said. "I mean, I beg your pardon? Carlos Pelayo doesn't live here? But this is the address on the computer at school."

"I have news for you," the woman said. "Computers aren't always right. Of course, if you had been born before television like I was, you might understand that."

"Are you sure, ma'am?" I asked, speaking for the first time.

"Of course, I'm sure," she said. "Seems like

most of the time computers make much bigger mistakes than humans do. I'm still fighting a utility bill that makes me just furious."

She scratched her dog's head. "Right, Sugar-booger?" she added in a high singsong voice.

Sugar-booger? "I mean about Carlos," I said, feeling like we'd walked into a movie shoot with the wrong script. "You're sure about him?"

She glared at me. "Are you asking me if I'm sure whether some kid named Carlos lives in my house? Like I'm some old lady who's lost her marbles?"

"I'm sorry," I said.

"You talk funny," she said. "I've never heard anyone say 'sore-ee.'"

"He's from Canada," Jennifer said. "They all sound funny up there."

Like that was helpful as we looked for Carlos?

"Canada?" she said. "My fifth husband was from Canada. But I'm not sure where. A stroke took him before I had time to find out much about him."

She scratched her dog's head again. "But he left behind lots of money, didn't he, Sugar-booger?" She frowned. "The Canadian dollar wasn't worth as much as I expected, and I almost felt cheated about the whole thing. His breath was horrible and—"

"We're sorry to have bothered you," I said, backing away.

Jennifer and I quickly walked to the car.

"I don't get it," she whispered. "My dad wouldn't make a mistake like this. He's the kind of guy who double-checks everything."

Before I could answer, we heard the woman say as she closed her door, "Come on, Sugar-booger. Time for our bath."

I shook my head. Wherever Carlos was tonight, I thought, he should be grateful not to be here.

Which, of course, left two obvious questions.

Where was Carlos?

And if Coach Lewis hadn't made a mistake, why did the computer have the wrong address?

chapter fourteen

At ten minutes after noon the next day, Jennifer and I followed Carlos Pelayo from room 225 to the school library. We stood by a drinking fountain down the hallway and watched him go in.

"So much for thinking we needed his entire schedule," Jennifer said. "This was way easier."

"Only because Mr. Johnson let us out of math five minutes early," I said. "Otherwise we wouldn't have had a chance to wait outside

Carlos's class. When the bell rings, it can be tougher getting through these hallways than to bust through a defensive line in football."

I should not have complained. The reason we'd been able to follow Carlos so easily was the crowded hallways. Staying out of sight had been easy.

I began to walk toward the library. Because we'd been standing still for a few minutes, I limped.

Jennifer noticed.

"What's the matter?" she asked.

"Nothing," I lied.

She looked at me with an odd expression. "I heard about Jason playing a trick on you, but I didn't want to believe it."

I shrugged. "It's my problem, all right?"

She didn't say anything.

"All right?" I repeated. I waited.

She finally nodded.

"All right," she said. She pointed at the library door. "We go in and find him?"

"That's right," I said. "It's a library. You know, quiet and boring. What can go wrong?"

* * *

What went wrong was the two guys with the black rose tattoos. They found Carlos first.

He was sitting in the corner by a window. Over his shoulder, I could see the chain-link fence outside the school. His face looked relaxed as he read the textbook in his lap. Beside him his leather jacket was folded neatly on the floor. He wore a white T-shirt, tight to his body. Without the leather jacket and without a scowl on his face, he looked a lot less tough, the way obnoxious little kids look sweet when they sleep.

Jennifer and I had just come around a bookshelf. It had taken us a few minutes of wandering the library to find Carlos. We moved slowly because we didn't want to just pop out of nowhere and scare him into leaving.

Neither of the guys with the tattoos noticed us near the bookshelf. They were focused on Carlos. Noticing a magazine rack that would keep us partly hidden, I grabbed Jennifer's arm to stop her from moving any farther. With my other hand, I put my finger in front of my lips to keep her quiet.

She raised her eyebrows.

"Met them earlier," I whispered. "His friends. This might not be a good time to visit Carlos."

Other students walked around, looking for books and talking with friends. Still, it seemed like there were just the five of us— Jennifer and me watching, Carlos reading and the two guys with tattoos.

Carlos didn't notice them until they stood in front of him and blocked the light from the window.

Carlos lifted his head. For a moment, it looked to me like a flash of fear crossed his face. Then he put on a big smile. A big fake smile.

Fear? I thought they were his friends and protectors.

The tattooed guys leaned forward and took turns speaking softly to Carlos. Jennifer and I were too far away to hear what they said.

Carlos shook his head. Once. Twice. Three times.

The smaller guy half-turned to hide what

he was doing. I didn't see much of what happened next, but I saw enough. He pulled a switchblade from his pocket and held it beneath Carlos's chin.

The bigger guy, standing tall, made a quick slitting motion across his throat with a finger.

"Did you see that?" Jennifer said.

"No," I said, "I did not see that knife. Knives are not allowed in the school. Remember, that's why they have metal detectors here. Therefore, what I saw could not have been a knife."

Jennifer knew I was being sarcastic. "What are you going to do about it?" she asked.

Carlos stood up.

"Do about what?" I replied, although I knew exactly what she meant.

"You can't let them threaten Carlos."

"You mean if I ask them nice," I whispered, "maybe they'll just go away and leave him alone?"

The smaller guy tucked the switchblade into his back pocket. They started to lead Carlos away from the window.

"If you're not going to stop them," Jennifer whispered, "then I will."

"Sure," I said. "Let me hold your purse while you beat them up for me."

She took a step toward them.

I groaned. I grabbed her arm as she tried to walk away.

"Wait here," I said. "Get ready to call nine-one-one. I'll need an ambulance."

I walked toward the small group.

All three turned their heads toward me.

"Hey, guys," I said.

"Beat it," the bigger guy said.

"I can't," I said. I spoke to Carlos. "You okay? You need help?"

He shook his head.

"You sure?" I asked. "I saw that guy pull a knife on you."

Both of the tattooed guys stepped toward me.

"Listen, jerk," the smaller one said, "we'll take you down right now. It'll happen so fast we'll be out of here before anyone notices your guts on the floor."

I was scared. But I was in this too far to back down.

"Just leave him alone," I said.

"Or what?" the big one sneered.

I didn't have a good "or what" to give him as an answer. I did my best to stare him down and show him I wasn't afraid. Although I was.

He took another step closer. I held my ground. I didn't look away.

He was so close that we could have bumped heads. His shiny brown eyes looked like snake's eyes.

Then, without warning, he stepped back.

"Okay," he said. "You win this one. But we'll be looking for you."

I hid my surprise, hardly able to believe that my tough guy act had worked. Especially since I'd never tried it before.

"Yeah?" I said, feeling braver. "Anytime you want, bring it on."

He didn't answer. He and his friend walked away.

Leaving me and Carlos, with Jennifer somewhere behind me.

I let out the breath I'd been holding.

Wow, I thought, I hope Jennifer caught all of that. Forcing those two to back down had been kind of impressive, even if I did say it myself.

"Hi," I said to Carlos, "glad we could help. It looked like you were in trouble there."

chapter fifteen

"You guys gone crazy?" His eyes were wide.

"They pulled a knife on you. What else were we going to do?" I was more than a little proud that they had just backed off. I wasn't going to mention that Jennifer had made me stand up to them. "And I wanted to talk to you."

"Man, you got any idea who they are?"

His words had this fast, cool rhythm.

"No. I'm new around here. My name is David Calvin."

Jennifer stepped up beside me.

"And this is Jennifer Lewis," I said.

I stuck out my hand, waiting for him to shake it and introduce himself, even though I already knew his name.

He ignored my hand. He didn't introduce himself.

Instead, Carlos Pelayo groaned. "Watch your back. That's all I can say. Watch your back. Nobody messes with those guys and gets away with it."

I shrugged. It wasn't like they would kill me or anything. I'd just make sure I stayed in places where there were other people around.

I dug into my pocket and pulled out some money.

"Here," I said. "This is yours."

He scrunched up his face, making it into a question mark.

"From the other day," I said. I explained the thing about the water pistol. I hoped he would find it funny.

He didn't laugh. And he didn't take the money.

"I don't get it," I said. "It doesn't matter that I didn't really pull a gun on you?"

"You don't get it," he said. "This isn't just about a few dollars. You think maybe you're the big hero, chasing me down to give this to me. But what you've done just makes things worse for me. You think I won't have to answer to those guys later?"

"Answer for what?" I asked.

He wiped all expression from his face.

"Nothing," he said. "Now, if you don't mind, I got to go."

"Look," I said. "If I can help you..."

"You've done enough," he said. He didn't mean it like a thank-you.

Jennifer finally spoke. "Carlos, my dad is a teacher here and the coach of the track team. He'd love it if you came out and ran for the Hurricanes. Maybe he can help—"

"The two of you are crazy. All I want is for you to leave me alone. You think maybe you can do that for me?"

I was slow to answer. So was Jennifer.

He took our silence to mean yes.

He walked away.

"Oh," I said to Jennifer. The money was still in my hand. "That sure didn't go the way I planned."

"You did your best," Jennifer said.

I brightened. "Yeah, at least I got rid of the other two. And in a hurry."

Jennifer shook her head. She held up a little plastic tube.

"Before you start thinking you're Superman," she said with a smile, "you'd better get one of these. You'll need it if they show up again."

I squinted.

"What is it?" I asked.

"Just breath spray," she answered with a grin.

"Oh," I said, "so I can attack their bad breath?"

She laughed at my confusion.

"No," she said, "but it also looks like mace. While you were playing tough guy, I walked up and held it behind your head. Like I was going to spray them. I figured guys who played with switchblades would assume I had mace. And I was right. They backed off in a hurry."

Wonderful. So much for being impressive. I had been rescued by a girl armed with breath spray.

chapter sixteen

Our doorbell rang and woke me up. It was still dark out. The bell rang three times, quickly, like someone was in a hurry to get the door answered.

I sat up. My alarm clock read five minutes past three. Who'd show up at five minutes past three in the morning?

I heard footsteps in the hallway. Heavy footsteps. Dad, not Mom.

It was so strange that I got out of bed and put on my jeans. I was used to phone calls in the middle of the night—Dad was a doctor. But who could be at the door?

I stepped into the hallway as I pulled on my sweatshirt. Dad was already walking back toward me.

"David," he said, "some kid is downstairs. Wants to talk to you. Says his name is Carlos."

Carlos?

I felt my heart bump into a higher gear.

Carlos. After school, I'd made sure I was never alone in the hallways, and I kept an eye out for those two guys with the tattoos. During practice, I'd hardly noticed my sore feet. I'd even secured my place to race on Saturday. But I'd spent most of my energy thinking and worrying about getting caught alone at some point. The only good thing was that some of the guys on the team had been friendlier to me. A couple had even pulled me into some of the joking around between sprints.

I hadn't seen Carlos's friends—if you could call them that—on the way home, even though I'd been watching for them. At suppertime,

I'd been so distracted that Mom asked me if something was wrong. If I had thought there might be something she could do to help, I would have told her. But it didn't seem right to get her worried about something I had to deal with, so I'd kept my mouth shut.

Even falling asleep, I'd been thinking about those two guys and wondering what hold they had over Carlos.

And now he was on our doorstep at three in the morning? It didn't make any sense to me.

"Who is he?" Dad asked.

"A guy from school," I said. "The one who thought I pulled a gun on him."

"I see," Dad said. His short hair stuck up in all directions. Much like mine probably did. "Guess you had a chance to talk to him. That explains why he knows where you live."

Then I realized something. All Carlos knew was my name. I hadn't told him where I lived. This was getting stranger by the second.

I followed Dad down the stairs.

We found Carlos bent over in the front

entry, leaning his hands on his knees. He was breathing heavy. Sweat popped from his forehead like he'd run to get here.

"Hi," I said.

He straightened and tried not to pant. "Remember today you said maybe you could help if I asked?"

I nodded. Dad was beside me.

"I came here because I got nowhere else to go. It's Juanita. My baby sister. I think maybe she's dying."

Carlos moved his dark eyes from my face to my dad's.

"You're a doctor. Can you save her?"

All I knew about Carlos was that he was proud and stubborn and, until now, had wanted me far away from his life. For him to be here and begging for help told me he was desperate.

Dad must have understood that. He didn't even hesitate.

"I'll get my coat and car keys," Dad said, "and tell your mother where we're going. You guys meet me at the car."

chapter seventeen

Dad carried a small leather bag filled with emergency medical equipment. And he was wearing a baseball cap. He threw one at me as he got into the car.

"Your hair looks goofy," he said. He tugged his hat down on his head. "And I'm afraid mine looks as bad as yours."

"Thanks," I said, not meaning it. Still, I put my hat on.

Dad started our Jeep Cherokee. He adjusted the rearview mirror to look at Carlos.

"Tell me where to go," Dad said, backing the Jeep into the street.

"You turn right at the corner."

Carlos gave Dad directions turn by turn. Other than that, we said little as we drove. It had rained during the night. The streets were oily wet, and as we passed beneath each streetlight, the drops of water on our windshield glinted like round diamonds.

Finally we reached a huge old house on a street near the school. Dad parked. We all got out.

Carlos walked ahead of us without a word.

We followed.

The grass had not been cut in weeks. As we walked up a crooked sidewalk, I saw bicycles buried in the yard like rusting skeletons. Ahead, in the shadows that fell on the house from a dim streetlight behind us, I saw that some of the windows were broken. There were few lights on inside the house.

It occurred to me to wonder if Carlos was taking us into some kind of trap.

Before I could say anything to Dad, we were at the front steps.

Then inside.

The air smelled stale. Like old garlic and grease. And cigarette smoke. And a little like a cat's litterbox. Somewhere deep inside the house a television blared.

Carlos flicked on a light.

We were in a hallway. I saw four doors, all shut, each with a name written on it in blue pen. Some names had been scratched out to make way for new ones.

I also saw a set of stairs leading up.

Carlos took the stairs.

I heard crying above us. I heard voices below from behind one of the doors. The stairs creaked. I was glad that Dad was here with me. We kept following Carlos.

At the top of the stairs, he turned on a bare bulb hanging from the ceiling. It brightened a long hallway to our right.

As we walked, I heard crying as we passed more doors with names scratched on them.

I finally figured it out. It looked like

this house had been turned into a bunch of tiny apartments.

I found out I was right when Carlos opened a door at the end of the hallway. A light was already on.

Dad and I stepped into the room behind Carlos.

We saw a man about Dad's age. A woman standing behind him clutched his arm. There were four children—two boys, two girls—all younger than Carlos, all wearing long T-shirts for pajamas.

Carlos said something quickly in Spanish to the man.

The man nodded and replied in Spanish.

"My father says thank you. He is honored you have chosen to visit us."

"Tell your father that my son and I are equally honored for the invitation."

Carlos translated, and then we all listened to his father speak again.

"My father says he has no money to pay for your help. But he promises to do whatever work you might have for him around your house."

"Tell your father I do not need money or repayment. Perhaps someday I can come to him with a request of my own."

Carlos passed that on to his father, who broke into a wide smile.

His mother tugged at his father's arm. She had a worried face. She said something to Carlos.

"My baby sister," Carlos said. "She is getting worse. She has become too weak to cry."

"Please take me to her," Dad said.

To me, Dad said quietly, "Wait here."

I did. Dad followed Carlos into another room. His father and mother went too.

That left me alone in what was both a living room and a kitchen. Alone except for the four little kids. They all stared at me as if I had landed from Mars.

Four little kids, a mother, a father, Carlos and a baby sister. Eight people living in two rooms. I saw five blankets with five pillows on the floor in this room; a sink, a stove and a fridge sat against the far wall. At the other side of the room was a table with two rickety chairs. There wasn't much else in the room except for an old sofa and a television with a broken antenna.

The little boys and girls kept staring at me.

I wiggled my eyebrows. They began to giggle.

I made a face, sticking out my tongue. They giggled more.

We were just becoming friends when Dad stepped out of the back room, holding a little bundle in a blanket. Carlos and his parents were close behind him.

"Come on," he said. "We're taking this girl to the hospital."

"No!" Carlos said. "You can't!"

His mother and father exchanged worried looks.

"She has a temperature of one hundred and three, her throat is swelling and she's dehydrated," Dad said. "I need to get some fluids into her fast."

"No hospital," Carlos repeated.

"Don't worry about the money," Dad said. "I'm a doctor there."

"No hospital."

Dad gave me the bundle to hold. I was surprised at how light it was. I saw a little of the baby girl's face. Hair stuck to her forehead. Her eyes were shut tight, with shiny stuff leaking from the corners of her eyelids. I thought of a helpless kitten, so young that its eyes hadn't opened yet.

Dad put his hands on Carlos's shoulders and faced him directly.

"I think I understand," Dad said. "Your parents don't speak English. You are in charge of the family. And you're afraid that someone at the hospital will start asking questions about how you all happen to be living here."

Carlos didn't say anything. But tears began to silently slide down his face.

"Son," Dad said gently, "I will do everything possible to protect this little girl. And your family. There's a nurse who will help us too. She and her family have faced the same problems you are."

Same problems? I wasn't sure what Dad meant. But I didn't get a chance to ask.

Carlos finally nodded.

"Okay," he said. "We go. We have to save Juanita."

chapter eighteen

Carlos and I sat in the emergency waiting room of the hospital. It was so quiet we could hear the electric hum of the clock on the wall. Like all hospital clocks, it was big and ugly, designed only to show the passing of time as clearly as possible. Time of hope or nervousness or fear. Time that people spent waiting for news—good or bad.

We had already spent half an hour alone while Dad worked with other doctors somewhere down the hall. Carlos had said nothing in that half hour.

I decided I wasn't going to break into his silence. I had plenty of questions for him, but this wasn't the right place. Not with him so clearly worried about his baby sister.

I stared at the hands on the ugly white clock. I was thinking about life, about how it didn't seem fair.

Why had Carlos been born into a family that had to share just two rooms? A family that couldn't even get medical help and had to send their oldest son to the hospital with a sick baby because he spoke English and his parents didn't?

Why had I been born into a doctor's family? A family where my brother and I had our own rooms? A family that could afford to send us to university?

Dad had once explained that the answer was less about what was or wasn't fair. It was more about life not always being fair and about helping people whenever we had the chance and...

"That was a funny thing," Carlos said,

interrupting my thoughts. "You with that pistol."

I blinked in surprise. That was the last thing I had expected him to say.

"Funny? I nearly got thrown in jail. And that wasn't the worst of it." I explained the part about the crap that I had rolled into.

For the first time, I saw Carlos smile. "Crap, like from a dog?" he asked.

"A big dog," I assured him. "A big dog that had eaten way too much."

He made a face and laughed. Long and hard. It was like once he got started laughing, he was using it as a way to get rid of all his worries. Even if just for a few minutes.

When he finally quit laughing, I spoke again.

"You run fast," I said. "You really should think about what Jennifer said. About running with the Hurricanes track team."

I thought about Carlos's family and how Dad had said Carlos was the one in charge. And I knew his family needed help.

"Maybe," I said, "you could get a track scholarship and go to university."

His face brightened. "That's what a person needs in America. Education. People who are born here think life is so easy. They don't take advantage of what they can do. People who are born outside, they would die for a chance like that." His face saddened. "And sometimes they do."

"What do you mean?" I asked.

"You probably figured it out by now," he said. "Me and my family, we're illegal."

Illegal. That's what Dad had meant when he said the nurse had faced the same problems Carlos faced. The big smiling nurse had told Carlos not to worry about the paperwork for now.

"Illegal," he repeated. "From Cuba. Even with the worst job, living here is ten times better than living where we did in Cuba. But some people don't make it across. I had a friend..."

His voice drifted off. His face got sadder. It didn't feel right to push him to finish.

He took a deep breath. "See, there are these people who promise to be guides, to take you across the ocean. They make you pay plenty.

Sometimes they take you across. Sometimes they just take your money. My friend and his family, they got in a boat. No one has seen them since. It's easy to throw someone off a boat out there—lots of water."

I shook my head in sympathy. I mean, what could a person say after hearing something like that?

"My father's dream," Carlos said, "is for all his children to grow up here. Become part of this country. Be citizens and have good jobs and freedom."

I finally understood why Carlos had not gone to the police when I'd taken his money. But it didn't explain why the school's computer had the wrong address for him. Or what was going on with those two guys with tattoos. And it didn't explain one other thing.

"Carlos," I said, "how did you know my dad was a doctor? And how did you know where I lived?"

He turned his dark eyes on me. "Please," he said. "Don't ask. For me and for you—you don't want to know."

"But—"

"No," he said, "listen. You talk to me about getting on the track team and trying for a scholarship. That would mean the world to me and my family. But there is no way I could do that. Not with where I am now and what I have to do to stay here. It is only a dream."

"But—"

"You can't even let anyone know I came to your house. If they find out, they will do terrible things to me and my family. Maybe to you too."

"They?"

"Please. I have already said too much." His mouth snapped shut.

I wanted to know so badly that I would have pushed him hard for an answer.

But I didn't have a chance.

Dad walked into the waiting room. He had dark bags under his eyes. And a big grin on his face.

"She'll be fine," he said to Carlos. "We brought her temperature down and gave her fluids. She's breathing easier, and the antibiotics seem to be working."

"Thank you," Carlos said quietly. "Thank you so very much."

He bit his lower lip, as if he was trying not to cry from relief.

I kept my questions to myself.

chapter nineteen

The school hallways were empty. Except for the two guys who had threatened Carlos in the library. Their footsteps echoed as they walked toward me. I backed away.

Then my feet got stuck. I looked down. My shoes were trapped in a puddle of black tar. I couldn't move.

The two guys got closer. They flashed their knives at me. Big knives with shiny blades.

I pulled at my feet. I still couldn't move.

I was desperate. I reached down and untied my shoes. I jumped sideways, landing clear of the tar. I turned and ran—and smacked into a wall that appeared from nowhere in the middle of the hall.

I was trapped!

I turned around again to face them.

They moved in closer and closer. They moved like zombies.

In my mind, I heard Carlos's words from the hospital waiting room: "You can't even let anyone know I came to your house. If they find out, they will do terrible things to me and my family. Maybe to you too."

"David...David," I heard. The voice was a low monotone, like a zombie's. In a weird way, I recognized the voice. It sounded like my math teacher. "David...David."

What kind of nightmare was this?

"David. David."

They brought their knives up to stab me. I screamed.

I threw myself to the side. The floor opened up beneath me. I felt myself falling. Screaming. Falling. Screaming.

Thunk!

I landed.

It hurt.

I opened my eyes. I was no longer in a hallway trapped by guys with knives. I was on the floor of my classroom. With my desk on top of me.

I'd been asleep?

"David."

It *was* my math teacher's voice. Mr. Johnson was standing over me. I saw his black shoes first and then his black pants. As I looked up, I saw his white shirt and black tie. Then his face. He was rolling his eyes in disgust.

I pushed myself to my feet. Everyone in the classroom had started giggling. I didn't dare look around. I hoped Jennifer wasn't laughing at me.

"If you want to sleep in class," Mr. Johnson said, "bring a pillow."

"Um. Yes, sir," I said. "I'm sorry. I was up late last night."

"Don't let it happen again."

"Yes, sir," I said.

He shook his head sadly. "And David?"

"Yes, sir?"

"Wipe that drool off your chin."

Since it was Friday, we didn't have track practice. Fridays were rest days, according to Coach Lewis. A day off, he said, gave our muscles a chance to rebuild and gave our blood sugars a chance to rise.

Instead of going to the gym right after school like I'd done since Tuesday, I went to the main office.

The secretary looked up at me from behind her desk. She had orange streaks in her hair and a round face. Her shirt was purple. She was maybe twenty-five, and she popped her gum as she chewed.

"Yeah," she said.

I pointed at the computer on her desk.

"I'm wondering if you could print out my registration information for me," I said.

"You don't know anything about yourself?" She popped a bubble.

"Yes, but I don't know about what's in the computer."

"You filled out the form when you registered, didn't you?"

"Yes," I said, "but—"

"So why do you need to see it again?"

I tried not to make a smart comment. "I just need to see it," I said.

"Got identification?" she asked, popping her gum again. She looked like she enjoyed making me work for this. "We have privacy laws, you know. How do I know you're not trying to find out about some other guy without his permission?"

I pulled out my wallet. I showed her my identification. She looked it over carefully. She studied the photo. She studied my face.

Finally she sighed. "All right then," she said. "It looks like I can't stop you."

You sure did your best though, I thought. I kept a polite smile on my face.

"Sit down," she said. "This is going to take a minute."

I sat down in the chair she pointed to. I stared at the clock and waited.

I'd had all day—except for my dumb nap

in math class—to think about this. Not that I should have been wasting any of my classroom time, but this whole thing with Carlos was too strange.

If his family was here illegally, how had he been able to register for school? I remembered all the paperwork I'd had to go through to register and get on class lists. I knew there was something strange going on. And for that matter, why had Carlos's address been wrong on the computer? How had he known my dad was a doctor? How had he known where to find me?

Jennifer told me after math class that she had not spoken to Carlos since our meeting in the library. So he hadn't learned about my family from her. The only thing I could think of was the school computer. Coach Lewis had been able to get personal information about Carlos from the computer. I figured maybe Carlos had somehow been able to get stuff about me.

This secretary had just answered one of my questions. I'd wondered how easy it was to get at another student's information. Now

I knew she wouldn't print out the information unless you had a photo ID.

That meant one of two things. Either Carlos had gotten stuff about me another way, without the computer system. Or he'd found another way to get into the school computer...

"Here you are," the secretary said, her gum snapping.

She looked over the printout before she handed it to me. "You aren't much of a rocket scientist, are you?"

I didn't get what she meant. At least, not until I read the printout.

What I read first didn't surprise me. At the top of the printout, I saw my address and what my parents did for a living. That told me that all Carlos had needed was the computer information to know where to find my doctor father and me. But it still didn't tell me how he had gotten into the computer.

Halfway down the page, I found out what the secretary had meant by her little insult about me not being a rocket scientist.

The printout listed all my high school

grades. None of the grades were from McKinley; I hadn't been here long enough. They were all the grades that had been transferred from my old high school.

And the grades were all wrong.

I was a B+ student.

All these grades showed me at D-.

Someone, somehow, had entered the computer system and changed them.

chapter twenty

Ten minutes later, I was staring at a black rose inside my locker, trying to figure out how it had gotten there. That's when my nightmare began to come true. I didn't see it coming in time to stop it.

My locker is at the far end of the school on the second floor. To reach it, I had to go down a narrow hall off the main hallway. Lockers lined both walls. I was completely alone when I found the rose.

I looked closer. It was a regular red rose,

but someone had spray-painted it black and put it inside my locker. In a weird way, it made sense. Whoever had read my computer file could have gotten my locker combination from it too.

But a black rose?

Behind me, I knew the narrow hall was empty, just like in my dream. Half an hour had passed since the final bell had rung. The school was like a tomb. Which wasn't a good setting for a nightmare.

I heard footsteps, just like I had in my dream.

When I made myself look up, they were there. The two guys who had threatened Carlos. The two guys with black roses tattooed on their arms.

Suddenly the rose in my locker made sense. Too much sense.

They walked toward me slowly, as if they had all the time in the world. Which they did. No one else was around.

They smiled. Not Welcome Wagon smiles. These were the smiles of wolves checking out a sheep who has wandered into a trap.

I began to back down the hall, away from them.

"Not so fast," the biggest one said. "Look behind you."

"Nice trick," I said. "Like I'm going to fall for that?"

"No trick, loser," a voice behind me said. "It's time to teach you a lesson."

I turned my head quickly.

Two more guys. Big. Leather vests. Ragged jeans. Black rose tattoos on their left biceps. They were blocking my way back to the main hallway. They too were walking toward me, moving slowly, smiles on their faces.

One of them had a cell phone. The other waved a switchblade.

"I don't get it," I said. "How do you guys get weapons into the school?"

"Easy," he said, kissing the blade with mock sweetness. "Someone tossed this one to me from outside. All I had to do was wait at the window we'd agreed on. Then I just hid it in my locker until I needed it."

"Good to know," I said, trying to sound brave.

The other guy spoke into his cell phone.

"We've got him here in the *A* wing," he said. "We'll bring him down the back stairs. Meet us there."

There were others?

My face must have shown my surprise.

"We have guys all over the school," the one with the knife said, answering my silent question. "Call it a network. A secret network. You can't get away from us."

This is what I knew from a self-defense course: The best time to resist is right away. If someone comes up to you in a parking lot and tries to force you into a car, the first thirty seconds are crucial. Once someone gets you into a car, you're in more trouble. Once that person gets you out of the city, you're in even bigger trouble. And so on. Resist loudly and publicly, and nine times out of ten, the bad guy will run away.

So I screamed as loud as I could.

Nobody ran away.

"Security guard's at the other end of the school," the guy with the cell phone said.

"Someone is watching him and will call me if he gets too close."

Oh.

So I did the next best thing.

I ran.

They thought there was nowhere for me to go. But there was one place they hadn't covered: the open door to a classroom right beside me.

I slammed the door shut. A desk was nearby.

In one motion I pulled it toward the door. I tilted it and wedged it under the handle just as they reached the door.

Through the door's window, I saw them laughing.

They weren't worried that I'd get away.

I heard the guy on the cell phone tell someone where I was.

One of the others rattled the handle. The door was stuck. He pushed hard and the door gave a little. I could see that the legs of the desk would probably slip on the waxed floor. I guessed I had less than thirty seconds to do something.

I ran to the desk at the front of the classroom. There was a telephone that I hoped was connected to the office. And I hoped the gum-snapping secretary was still there.

I picked it up.

It dialed automatically.

It rang.

No answer.

Three rings. Four. Five...

The desk slipped, and the door opened slightly as all four guys pushed.

I dropped the phone and ran to the window.

The school grounds were nearly empty. This wasn't the type of place kids hung around if they didn't have to.

I looked down. I didn't like what I saw. Two long stories down to the bushes that grew along the building.

But more banging at the door made me act.

I opened a window.

I stuck my head out and looked to the right.

A drainpipe!

The rusted drainpipe was easily within my reach. Even if I only had time to crawl halfway down, I could get close enough to the ground to jump safely.

Bang! Bang! Bang!

They almost had the door open wide enough to get in.

I couldn't wait. I stretched out to reach the drainpipe, hoping it would hold my weight. I got my hands on it and let my body slide out the window.

It held! So far, so good.

I began to lower myself, scraping my knees and elbows against the rough sandstone wall.

Five seconds later, I heard voices above me.

I expected someone to reach out to try and shake the drainpipe. I was still too far off the ground to jump. All I needed was five more seconds.

Then I heard the guy on the cell phone.

"Call them in from all points," he said calmly from above me. "Get them to the back of the school. He's climbing down the wall. You should be able to trap him on the ground."

All points? How many were there?

I found out seconds later.

Halfway down the drainpipe, I looked around. The once-empty grounds outside the school were no longer empty.

At least a dozen guys were jogging toward me from different corners of the school.

chapter twenty-one

I didn't have much choice. I had to get to the
ground as quickly as possible. I scooted down
the drainpipe a few more feet.

I checked the ground.

I was right above a bush.

As I pushed off the drainpipe, I caught the
edge of the bush and rolled onto the grass.
Then I scrambled to my hands and knees.

It didn't feel like I had broken any bones.
That was the good news.

The bad news was that three guys were

already so close I didn't have a chance. I couldn't possibly get up and run before they caught me.

Then there was the other bad news. It was a smell I wished I didn't recognize. I looked down.

Sure enough, my nose had not lied. Half of it was still on the grass beneath me. The other half was smeared on my shirt.

What was it with Florida dogs? Were they all huge and able to eat like elephants? And do other stuff like elephants?

I raised my head again. Two guys stood right in front of me.

I knew a third one was behind me. That wasn't hard to figure out after I felt him kick me.

"Get up," one of them said. "It's time for a talk."

Farther away, I could see that the others had slowed down. After all, now that I was trapped there was no reason to run.

The guy behind me kicked me again. I didn't really think they wanted to talk.

I could think of only one thing to do.

I really didn't want to do it. I mean, if I'd had any luck, I would have landed in a place where I could scoop sand or dirt in my hands and throw it in their faces to give me a chance to get away.

But, of course, there was no sand or dirt. I was on grass.

That left me only one thing to throw in their faces.

I brought my hands together as I got ready to stand. My head and shoulders hid what my hands were doing. I grabbed the weapon that the big dog had left me. A scoop in each hand.

I stood up.

And I threw with all my might at the two guys in front of me.

It splattered in their faces, covering their eyes and noses.

While they were blinded, I took my chance. I bolted forward, hoping to leave them in the dust shouting about what had hit them in the face.

But the guy behind me managed to get a hand on my shirt. He spun me around and grabbed my shoulders. I stood face-to-face with a wide-shouldered kid with dark hair and angry eyes.

I reached out, wiping both of my hands across his face, catching mainly his mouth and chin.

He dropped his hands from my shoulders, gagging and spitting, which gave me some open space.

I took it.

My feet still hurt a bit from where the tacks had poked through my shoes, but I hardly felt the pain. I ran at full speed, aiming for a gap that was quickly closing as the others moved to cut me off.

They didn't have a chance.

They weren't running for their lives—I was.

The closest any of them came to me was five yards. Then I was past them all, out in the open field. It became a foot race, with me leading about eight or nine guys.

I headed for the far corner of the grounds, about two hundred yards away. I had seen an opening someone had cut in the chain-link fence. By the time I reached it, my lead had increased to fifty yards.

I burst through the opening. I had two choices. Right or left. Up the street or down. Up the street toward houses and trees and yards and parked cars. Or down the street toward stores and parking lots and restaurants.

I decided to head up the street. I hoped the guy with the cell phone didn't have other people hiding up there.

I pushed hard, pounding along the sidewalk. The more I ran, the less my feet hurt.

It was so good to be free, I didn't even care about the smell that filled my nostrils with every deep breath I took.

Now all I had to do was find a safe place to hide. And a place to wash my hands.

chapter twenty-two

As I ran, I wondered if I should call the police. The guys behind me were falling farther and farther back. In a few minutes, I would be far enough away to cut into a yard, come out the other side somewhere and disappear. That would give me time to find a telephone.

But all I'd be able to tell the police was that some guys had been chasing me. "To do what?" the police would ask. "I don't know," I'd have to say. "I didn't let them catch me."

"So what do you expect us to do?" the police would ask.

"I don't know," I'd have to say. "Can you ask them to leave me alone?" And the police would laugh at me like I was a little crybaby.

I reached a corner and turned hard. I'd settled into a fast jog, and my lungs and legs were getting into a good rhythm. I wasn't worried about running out of energy anytime soon. I was more worried about Monday, when I returned to school. After all, how often could I escape from these guys? And for that matter, what had I done wrong? And what was this network thing about? Spies everywhere in the school? Connected by cell phones?

I turned another corner, cut through a yard and jumped a low hedge. It took me into another yard. I saw a hose stretched into a flower bed with the water running.

I stopped. My chest was heaving for air, but I wasn't in pain.

I reached out for the water, scrubbing my hands together, cleaning them as quickly as I could.

I looked back but saw no signs of anyone. I hoped they had given up, but I wasn't going to take a chance.

I put my thumb over the end of the hose to shoot water at the front of my shirt. The water was cold and made me gasp. But I kept spraying, trying to drive off as much of the stuff as I could. I was sure I'd have to throw the shirt away, like I had the other one. But at least I wouldn't have the stuff clinging to me as I went home.

Still no sign of anyone. I began jogging again, slipping out the back of the yard and onto a different street.

As I ran, I passed an old rusting Cadillac parked by the curb. The back window was smashed out. The rear bumper was totally crunched. I remembered it from the night before, when Dad and I had gone to Carlos's house.

I had found Carlos's neighborhood again.

Still running hard, I looked more closely at the houses on each side of the street. With the sun shining bright in a cloudless sky, the street looked very different from the way it had the night before. I recognized some of the houses. A half block later, I stood in front of the big old house where Carlos and his family lived.

I stared at the huge house with its broken windows. Clothes hung from balconies to dry in the breeze.

I told myself this had all started with Carlos. If he was the problem, then he might also be the solution.

I ran up the front walk. I pushed the door open, smelling the same scent of garlic and grease from the night before, hearing the same loud television from somewhere on the main floor. As I walked up the stairs, I heard babies crying somewhere above me. I walked down the hallway and passed the same doors with the same chipped and peeling paint.

I stopped in front of the door that led to Carlos's family's two-room apartment.

I knocked and waited.

chapter twenty-three

Carlos opened the door. He didn't say a thing.

He looked up and down the hallway. Ignoring my soaking-wet T-shirt, he pulled me inside and bolted the door behind me.

"You must be crazy," he said. "What you doing here? Man, people see us together, I'm dead."

His brothers and sisters wandered out of the small bedroom at the back of the apartment. They stared at me. They spoke to one another in Spanish. Probably talking about my wet T-shirt.

His father and mother weren't here. Or if they were, they stayed in the other room.

"I'm here because I don't want to have to worry about getting knifed at school," I said. "The people you hang with aren't too nice. And for some reason, they don't like me."

"They don't like you because you put your nose where it don't belong. Just like now." He sniffed the air. "Man, speaking about noses..."

He sniffed again. "Is that what I think it is?"

"How's your little sister?" I asked. I didn't want to answer his question.

"Better," he said. He sniffed again. "What do you do? Look for that stuff and roll in it? Are you some kind of sick?"

"Some kind of unlucky. And again, it's your fault."

"Me? I don't push you into it. I don't—"

"You looked me up in the school computer, didn't you?" I looked squarely into his face. "When you saw my dad was a doctor, you decided to visit because Juanita was sick."

"It wasn't me," he said. "It was them. I just overheard them talking about you and your family and where you lived."

"'Them'?" I asked. "Who is 'them'?"

He didn't answer.

"They changed my grades too, didn't they? Who are they? And how do they get into the system?"

"No," he said, shaking his head, "I can't tell you anything."

"There are guys with black rose tattoos chasing me. You've got to tell me what's going on."

"No way," he said. He pointed at his brothers and sisters. "You say the Black Roses be chasing you. That's your problem. I can't let you put your problem on my family."

The Black Roses.

"The Black Roses?" I said. "Is that the name of a gang?"

"You stupid?" he asked. "You live all your life in some igloo? Of course the Black

Roses are a gang. They rule the school, man. All of it."

"Then I really need your help," I said.

"So that's it," he answered. "You're here because you think I owe you for what your old man did for my sister."

"No," I said, "that's between my dad and you. I'm asking for your help because I don't know where else to start. Tell the Black Roses I don't have a fight with them."

"Me?"

"They'll listen to you. You're part of them."

"They don't listen to no one. And I'm trying to stay out of it too."

What?

"I don't get it," I said. "If you're not part of them..."

"I can't tell you nothing," he said. "How many times I gotta say that? I'm in too deep."

He stared at me. I stared at him.

In too deep.

I wondered if I should tell Carlos about

my dad. And how he once thought he was in something too deep.

I decided I would tell him. I drew a breath to speak.

The door behind us opened. It banged against the chain lock.

"Carlos?" It was a woman's voice.

Carlos spoke Spanish to her. He unlocked the chain and opened the door. His mother walked in, holding a bag of groceries.

The first thing I noticed was a black rose sticking out of the bag. Just like the rose I had found in my locker. Whatever color it once had been, it was now spray-painted black.

Carlos saw it too. He pointed at it and spoke some urgent Spanish to his mother. She smiled and explained something.

All the life left Carlos's face. His shoulders slumped.

"What is it?" I asked.

"She said she was walking home when this nice boy came up and gave her the rose."

Carlos could barely speak. "It's a message.

To me. I'm now on their list. And they want me to know they can get me anytime. And that they can get to my family."

"If that's true," I said, "then you have no choice. You have to do something—now."

He looked at the floor for a long time. He finally looked up at me again. He nodded.

"Maybe we can help each other," I said. "But you have to tell me what's going on."

After a few seconds, he nodded again.

chapter twenty-four

Just my luck, I had to run into the two policemen who had stopped me with my brother's water pistol.

I was sitting in the police station, three hours after talking to Carlos. I'd had a chance to go home and change my shirt. I was waiting for another officer to come out and talk to me. I saw the big cop with the mustache first. Then his partner caught up to him.

They caught me looking at them. They

were so close that I could read the names on their badges. Fernetti. Tunnerd.

They stopped.

Fernetti, the one with the mustache, snapped his fingers.

"You," he said. "You're the kid who rolled in the—"

"Yes," I said. How long was that going to follow me? At least they didn't know about the second time. "That's me."

"Robbed anyone with a water pistol lately?" Tunnerd asked. They both laughed.

"No," I said, "but I found out why the boy I was chasing ran away. And that's why I'm here."

"Yeah?" They were still laughing.

"He thought I was in the Black Roses," I said.

That stopped their laughter.

"What do you know about the Black Roses?" Fernetti asked.

I shook my head. "Not until I have a deal."

"Deal?" Tunnerd said. "What do you think this is? Television? You don't get no deal."

They moved closer, looking down on me. Both of them had their hands on their billy clubs.

"Tell us what you know, kid. And don't mess with us."

Fortunately I saw Dad heading down the hallway. A woman in uniform walked with him. They reached me as the two cops in front of me were pushing closer.

"Fernetti. Tunnerd," the woman said. Her dark blue uniform was crisply ironed. Her blond hair was pulled back in a bun. There was no smile on her face or in her voice. "What are you doing?"

They backed away.

"Kid's got something to tell us about the Black Roses," Tunnerd said. "And he's trying to get cute and cut some deal."

"He does have a deal," she snapped. "And he's got a lot to say. Since it's your neighborhood, how much of it do you want to hear?"

"All of it," Fernetti said.

"Then behave." She smiled. "Better yet, apologize for trying to push him around."

We all sat in her office. I knew her name from the sign on her door: *Captain Helen Chandler*. On her desk was a picture of her with her family.

She'd had the officers bring some chairs in from another room. It was crowded, but I didn't mind.

"Dr. Calvin was kind enough to explain quite a bit to me before you two joined us," Captain Chandler said, her words as crisp as her uniform. "And I have agreed to his terms. Which means you can proceed, David."

So I told them what had happened to me during the week, right down to the part where I was chased from the school. When I told them about not having sand to throw when I was trapped, I thought they'd never stop laughing.

"What my friend told me was this," I finally broke in. "The Black Roses have a hacker, someone who can get in and out of computer systems without getting caught. Or noticed."

"Computer systems?" Fernetti said. "What good does that do to a bunch of punks in a high school gang?"

"Bank computers," Captain Chandler explained. "Utility company computers. Military computers. How dangerous do you think someone would be who can get into them?"

Fernetti whistled. "Plenty."

"Except they stay away from those computers," I said. "At least, from what I know."

"Meaning?" Captain Chandler asked.

"Meaning they might not be able to make money getting into those computers."

"Bank computers...," Fernetti said. "Wouldn't tapping into them be like breaking into a bank?"

I nodded my head. "But sooner or later, banks will notice the money is missing. Someone will come looking. Even if they never catch you, you'd always be worried about that possibility. And selling military secrets would be dumb too. Then you're dealing with people from other countries. And you wouldn't want two armies after you."

"You seem to know a lot," Tunnerd said. "You sure you're not the 'friend' you're talking about?"

"I'm not the friend," I said. "I just like reading books and learning about computers and stuff."

Which was why I had gone to the school secretary in the first place. I'd wondered if computers were involved in some way.

"How can we be sure you're not the friend?" Tunnerd asked.

"Because my family moved to Florida legally."

"Huh?" he asked.

"The Black Roses get their money from people in their neighborhoods. People they know they can scare. People they've helped move here. People who can't go to the police for help because, if they do, they'll get kicked out of the country."

"Illegal immigrants, right?" Captain Chandler asked. "This is about illegal immigrants."

I nodded, thinking of Carlos and his family and how they were struggling to survive.

"When the Black Roses hack into computers, they don't steal anything. Because when you take something, the people who own it eventually come looking. Instead they add things."

Captain Chandler nodded as she began to understand what Carlos had explained to me. With millions of names on computer databases—like the ones for the school systems in Florida—who's really going to notice if you add a few more? Or a few dozen more? Or even a few hundred more?

"In a few months," I said, "my friend and his family will be US citizens. At least the government computers will show them to be citizens. The hacker has even enrolled my friend and other people like him in school, just by breaking into the main computer system for the city's school district."

I explained the rest of it. How the Black Roses not only made money by selling citizenships and entry into the education systems but also by taking their time getting the citizenship stuff cleared. In the meantime, they blackmailed people like Carlos into doing stuff for them. If, like Carlos, those people tried to say no, the Black Roses would threaten them or their families, knowing they would never go to the police.

"Wow," Fernetti said. "That's big business. You almost have to be impressed that high school kids can have so much power."

"This is bigger than you think," I said. "From what my friend tells me, it's not just the Black Roses. It looks like they're the muscle for someone else."

Captain Chandler, Fernetti and Tunnerd all leaned forward.

"There's someone at the top who sets this up for different gangs in different areas," I said. "If someone can break into computer systems, why stop at one neighborhood?"

"In other words," Captain Chandler said, "stopping the Black Roses is like cutting off one branch. To get the whole tree, we need to get to the root—the hacker and whoever he works for."

I nodded.

This was why Carlos had been so scared. And why I was in so much trouble for getting involved. Because the whole tree was so big, and so much money was at stake.

"We definitely can't do this ourselves," the captain said. She picked up the phone and punched some numbers. She waited for a few seconds.

"Yes," she said when someone answered on the other end, "I need to speak to someone in the FBI's computer crimes division."

chapter twenty-five

Saturday morning. Eight o'clock. Clear, deep blue sky. Grass wet with heavy drops of dew. No traffic. Most of the track team stood in the parking lot behind the school, waiting beside an old yellow bus that would take us across town for the track meet.

I was standing by myself. Other people had clustered in small groups. There was no sign of Jennifer and her dad yet. That, of course, was why we were waiting.

Jason walked toward me.

As usual, he had a sneer on his face.

"Heard the Black Roses are after you," he said.

"News travels fast," I said.

"You might as well leave the school," he said. "Once they decide to get you, they'll never quit."

"That's what I understand," I said.

Jason and I were in our own little world. The early sun cast our shadows on the side of the bus.

"Aren't you scared?" he asked. For a second his sneer dropped, as if he was really curious about why I wasn't scared. For a second I almost liked him.

"Sure I am," I said. "Is that what you want? Or do you need me to show it too?"

"Me?" He put the sneer back on his face. "Why should I care?"

"That's my question, I guess. Why should you care? Why have you done your best to make things tough on me? I never once did anything to you."

He spat on the ground in front of me. "You're a Christian."

"Huh?" I wasn't surprised he called me that; I wore a silver cross on a chain around my neck. What did surprise me was the anger and hatred in his voice.

"Christians." He repeated it with the same anger and hatred, and he spat on the ground again. "A Bible-thumper like you comes along and Jennifer gets taken in by how nice she thinks you are."

Bible-thumper? That wasn't me. My dad always quotes a writer named Augustine: "Go out into the world and preach; if necessary, use words." That was the whole reason Dad had moved us down here: so he could work in the clinic. He believed that what you did counted way more than what you said.

I hadn't once tried to force Jason or anyone else to believe what I believed.

"My old man calls himself a regular Christian," Jason continued. "Before he and my mom split up, he used to hit me. He said it was his duty to drive the devil out of me. Sometimes he hit my mom too. When she left him, he told me I was going to hell because I wanted to live with her instead of him. And he hasn't paid a cent of alimony. That's why I have to go to a dump of a school like this."

I felt so bad for Jason, I almost put my hand on his shoulder. But the look of hatred on his face told me he didn't want kindness from me.

"Ever thought maybe your dad was wrong?" I asked.

"Whatever," he said. He spat once more and began to turn away.

"Jason," I said, "this sounds dumb, but I'm going to do my best to help you."

He turned back, a look of disbelief on his face. "Help me? That's a good one. With the Black Roses after you, you're the one who needs help."

I'd thought I would enjoy this morning. I had no doubt Jason had put the tacks in my shoes. And Jason had turned people against me. I'd thought revenge would make me feel good. But I hadn't known about his dad. And he, of course, didn't know about mine.

"Let me tell you about my dad," I said. Coach Lewis and Jennifer were due to show up any second. So I spoke quickly.

"He is a great doctor," I said. "He made good money. Everybody liked him. He didn't beat us up or anything. It was the opposite. He left us alone. He just worked and worked and made money and gave us things instead of his time."

"Poor boy," Jason said. "I can see how life has treated you bad. Brand-new bikes and televisions and stuff like that. Ouch. Ouch. Ouch."

"Listen," I said, "the long days and stress got to him. He did something that's too easy for any doctor to do. He started prescribing drugs to himself. Pretty soon that wasn't enough. Once he was hooked, he started stealing drugs from the hospital because if he prescribed as much as he wanted, people would know what was happening. Then he discovered cocaine. Six months of it cost our family nearly everything we owned. It ripped our life apart."

I had Jason's attention.

"When my dad was at his lowest," I said, "he finally figured out that he had turned to cocaine because he wanted something to fill his emptiness. When he started looking for answers, the emptiness gradually went away."

"Just like that," Jason said. "Say your prayers and everything's all better."

"No," I said, "it was a long way back for him. And for our family. He went into rehab and had to be certified as a doctor again. But he found purpose. And peace." I paused to take a breath.

"Look," I said, "could it hurt to at least think about what I'm saying?"

I could see that Jason was considering what I had said.

I could also see past him. I watched as a car with three people in it drove up the street to the parking lot. A police car followed.

chapter twenty-six

I was nearly out of time.

"Jason," I said, "the Black Roses had you join the track team so you could pretend to make friends with Coach Lewis. You figured out he doesn't know much about computers."

His face darkened. "What of it?" he said.

"I'm trying to help you," I said. "Listen. Please."

The cars arrived at the entrance of the

parking lot and began to turn in. Jason still hadn't seen them.

"You needed access to one school system computer," I said. "You needed a back door."

"You're nuts," he said.

"No," I said, "I was there last night when they trapped you."

"Trapped me? Who?"

I hadn't understood any of the technical details. What I'd seen looked like a cat and mouse game on a computer screen. The computer programmer had explained it to me as he chased the hacker.

"You made sure Coach Lewis's computer was always available by modem," I said. "You had his password and broke into McKinley's system. You put three hacked accounts between your home computer and Coach's computer. But last night, someone followed every move you made in the school's system, keystroke by keystroke."

Hacked accounts. That was something else I had learned about from the programmer. They were other people's computer accounts, which the hacker broke into. It was kind of like using someone else's car to rob a bank so the license plate would get traced back to the owner instead of the bank robber.

I'd watched the computer screen over the programmer's shoulder. The hacker never knew he'd been caught. Every keystroke he made showed up on our screen. He'd entered new names and addresses, and then he'd changed grades to help other students pass their classes. Most of those other students were Black Roses members. I'd watched as the programmer had followed the hacker out of the system and right to his home computer. Almost like putting a homing device inside the bag of money stolen by a bank robber. It wouldn't matter how many different cars he used as he drove away.

The hacker's trail led us to Jason's home computer. Jason, who didn't like me because of the cross I wore around my neck. Jason, who didn't like me because I was becoming friends with Jennifer. Jason, who had learned a lot about me from my school records. Jason, who had told his Black Roses friends about me. And what to do about me.

"Jason," I said, "they know it's you. They picked this morning to serve a search warrant on your house because they knew you'd be here, waiting to get on the bus. Whatever evidence you have on your computer's hard drive, they now have."

"Impossible," he said. The look on his face told me otherwise.

"When the police get here," I said, "help them as much as you can. They'll go easier on you. You're still young enough that this won't hurt you for the rest of your life."

He saw me looking over his shoulder. He whirled his head and caught a glimpse of the cars pulling up—Coach Lewis and the police.

For a second, Jason tensed. Like he was thinking of running. Then his shoulders slumped.

Jason looked back at me.

"The guy who tracked you last night," I said, "he used to be a hacker too. Until he decided to take what he knew about computers and use it to help keep systems secure."

The cars were very close. Close enough that I could see the faces of Coach Lewis and

Jennifer in the first car. And a third person in the backseat.

"Jason," I said, "from what they were saying about you, you're a computer genius. Just like my dad, you can turn things around."

I didn't have a chance to say more. The cars stopped. Kids on the track team backed away and watched in silence as the officers from the second car came over to talk to Jason.

He gave me a long look.

"Remember," I said, "I'll help if you want."

"All right," he finally said.

They ushered him away from the team to talk to him in private.

By then Coach Lewis and Jennifer had gotten out of their car.

"Wow," Coach Lewis said, letting out a deep breath. "What a morning. I've been up for hours, talking with police and school officials."

I looked at the back of his car, where the third person was still sitting.

"Carlos is here," I said. "Does that mean the police kept their end of the deal?"

chapter twenty-seven

Coach Lewis smiled. "The police honored their deal. Carlos agreed to testify against the Black Roses. That, along with the computer evidence, should be enough to get the gang out of the school and into the court system. That's going to make life a lot easier on everyone. In return for his help, the FBI will get Carlos's family what's called political asylum. That means they can stay in the United States legally."

"And if Jason decides to help the FBI too," I said, "they'll have a real head start on finding out who is organizing this from neighborhood to neighborhood."

I thought to myself that I wouldn't be surprised if Jason did help. It would be the only way for him to stay out of a lot of legal trouble. And just before the police put him into their car, I saw that he looked more scared than angry. Maybe he was thinking about the things I'd told him.

Coach's car door opened. Carlos got out. He was dressed in track sweats with our school colors. Carlos gave me a big thumbs-up. And an even bigger grin.

"Carlos is running for us today." I guessed.

"Yup," Coach Lewis said. "I called the other sprinters this morning to see if they could run in Jason's place. But neither of them could make it on such short notice. That means Carlos gets to be our fifth runner today."

I thought about what Carlos had said about getting a scholarship and going to a university. I thought about how fast he was. And how this chance to run might be his first step in his journey toward his dream.

I walked over to him.

"You feel good?" I said.

"You bet, man."

He grinned again, jogging in place to warm up his legs. "Tell you what. This is like a door opening for me and my family. I feel sorry for whoever runs against me today."

That meant he needed to feel sorry for me.

Everything came down to the final sprint. Carlos had qualified. So had I. And runners from four other schools.

We needed to finish first and third to give Coach Lewis his first victory in a long time.

The crowd was loud as we took our places. Big as the crowd was, I found Jennifer easily. She gave me a shy wave when she noticed me looking at her. Then she blew me a kiss. I didn't know where to look.

Carlos had taken his place at the blocks beside mine. He elbowed me.

"You make pretty eyes later," he said. "Now you get ready to chase me."

"Me chase you?" I said in mock astonishment.

He grinned. "You bet. I'm going to be ahead of you all the way to the finish line."

I had a smart remark but no time to fire it at him. The starter called us to the starting blocks.

I crouched. For a second, time froze. The sun warmed my back. With my head up, the view etched into my mind. People in the stands. Some palm trees at the edge of the field. A blue cloudless sky.

And my legs ready to burn.

"Take your mark..."

The starter raised his pistol.

"Set..."

BANG!

I was liquid mercury as the gun shot its blank.

Legs churning. Track hard against my feet.

A rush of air and motion and the blur of colored uniforms.

Two guys ahead. Then one. Into the lead. Closing in on the finish line.

I felt free. A hawk diving. A shark slicing through water. A cheetah in tall grass.

Almost at the line.

But just before I burst across, Carlos charged out of nowhere, past my right shoulder. And across the line.

For a second, I was crushed. But only for a second. Then I realized what had happened. We'd finished first and second!

Above the screaming of the crowd, I heard the announcer's voice on the loudspeaker.

"Folks! An unofficial record! That's the fastest high school time in Florida by at least a tenth of a second! The first and second places both broke the old record!"

Carlos pounded my back.

I pounded his.

The rest of the team swarmed us.

So how could I be upset?

Especially with Coach Lewis almost

crying from happiness at his first win in years.

Beside, there was always next week's race to catch Carlos. This time without a water pistol in my hand.

Orca Sports

All-Star Pride
Sigmund Brouwer

Blazer Drive
Sigmund Brouwer

Cobra Strike
Sigmund Brouwer

Hitmen Triumph
Sigmund Brouwer

Hurricane Power
Sigmund Brouwer

Jumper
Michele Martin Bossley

Kicker
Michele Martin Bossley

Rebel Glory
Sigmund Brouwer

Tiger Threat
Sigmund Brouwer

Titan Clash
Sigmund Brouwer

Two Foot Punch
Anita Daher

Winter Hawk Star
Sigmund Brouwer

Visit www.orcabook.com for more Orca titles.

Sigmund Brouwer is the best-selling author of many books for children and young adults. He has contributed to the Orca Currents series (*Wired, Sewer Rats*) and the Orca Sports series (*Blazer Drive, Titan Clash, Cobra Strike*). Sigmund enjoys visiting schools to talk about his books.

Interested teachers can find out more by e-mailing authorbookings@coolreading.com.